DISCARDED
BUSINESS IS BALONEY

By

Leo T. McCall

This book is a work of fiction. Places, events, and situations in this story are purely fictional. Any resemblance to actual persons, living or dead, is coincidental.

© 2002 by Leo T. McCall. All rights reserved.

No part of this book may be reproduced, stored in a retrieval system, or transmitted by any means, electronic, mechanical, photocopying, recording, or otherwise, without written permission from the author.

ISBN: 0-7596-8230-5

This book is printed on acid free paper.

Printed in the United States of America

1stBooks - rev. 1/17/02

For information regarding this title, please contact:
Leo T. McCall
515 South Lexington Parkway, #106
St. Paul, MN 55116
(651) 699-8458

THE AUTHOR WISHES TO THANK

George J. Kronschnabel
A Very successful business man and that is
No baloney

Ann Keller of Meredith, New Hampshire, for her
Excellent work in editing this novel

His friend, Randall Birkel, for his comments on
Reading the advance copy

Mr. Birkel and the author worked side-by-side at Brown and Bigelow right after the end of World War II. Here is what he wrote after reading *Business is Baloney*:

"Thanks. A very interesting and humorous publication. I read it twice. It kept me in stitches it was so fascinating."

Randall J. Birkel

Randall J. Birkel

Table of Contents

ONE
The Barbecue 1

TWO
Wire Reports 13

THREE
Miami Bound 23

FOUR
Montana Mission 31

FIVE
The Macknighter 53

SIX
Down on the Farm 61

SEVEN
Choose, Hamilton and Loose 69

EIGHT
Reunion at the Como Zoo 70

NINE
Goal Line Stand 81

TEN
The Funeral and the Will 85

LIST OF CHARACTERS

CHARLES FOXWORTH AKA "FOXIE": Original "Bus Boy" armed always with a shoeshine kit—tooth brush and lint brush bag—combs and brushes plus chauffeur's license

JOHN REGO AKA "SHAKESPEARE": Corncob pipe smoker—red flannel jacket wearer—4" wide belt buckle—initial "R". Eyes and ears of Hall & Hall…well informed—well-read on Wall Street Journal, New York Times, Harry Hall's Ghost Writer

FUSS FENDER AKA "RAZZ-MA-TAZZ": Sparkling smile, bouncy walk, can do man, always the cheerleader, tap dancer at parties, girl whistler, back slapper, hog caller, throttle always wide open, fancy dresser, expensive suits, motto, look prosperous and you'll be prosperous

STUMP HARRIGAN: Hand shaker, moocher, baby kisser, girl watcher, and funeral attender when Harry couldn't make it, did anything to get attention…never needed a drum

LES JAMES AKA "PREACHER": Bean counter, bible quoter, lethargic, uninspiring, hates salesmen (all sinners to Les)…kept salesmen honest by watching their expense accounts…moved as slow as a turtle expert when Harry called

HARRY HALL "THE BOSS": Loud, bombastic, fearless, egotistic, uneducated liked the applause of the underlings, paid them well, knew nothing about selling his glue but sure knew hot to get his salesmen to see it…"scare the hell out of them"

ONE

The Barbecue

Overhead, a shapely imported Italian model swung lazily on a swing inside a golden bird cage. The cage, at least six feet in diameter, hung on a golden chain from two gold-sprayed beams. Actually, the cage should have been silver, honoring Harry's 25th Silver Jubilee. But Harry had once heard of a bird in a gold, gilded cage. The girl, dressed in glove-fitting gold tights, swung side-saddle—her long, dark curly h air entangling occasionally with the golden chains. She nibbled hors d'oeuvres handed up to her by an ever changing group of stiff-necked admirers. While the admirers, in the main, were mostly ordinary, the hors d'oeuvres certainly were not.

Fresh shrimp direct from the shrimp boats of New Orleans was flown in on Branigg's first-class, non-stop Imperial, red carpet Champagne Flight 703. Canary tongue, (not flown in) was delivered in person by an emissary from Uruguay, who slaughtered half his canary collection for the occasion, tasted delectable. Buffalo tips from Harry's private herd (now made extinct by the festive occasion) certainly would have been approved by Duncan Hines, himself. The usual jumbo herring, Wisconsin cheddar cheese, Seattle canned clam chowder, plus Atlantic shark meat satisfied the most discriminating palates.

Milk for ulceric District Managers couldn't have been fresher. The pride of Harry's Holsteins, cornered in a stall next to the Blacksmith Shop, produced happily while being milked by an ambidextrous milkmaid, who, you can be sure, was no gal born down on the farm. One of Harry's top District Managers was heard to say that he attributed his loss of weight (and what appeared to be top physical condition) to the fact that he drank

Leo T. McCall

only milk—nothing else. Other envious managers, not in favor with Harry at the time, said that because of the tremendous pressure he had on himself and his men, he could hold nothing else on his stomach.

A bar, extending roughly the length of a football field, was constructed to enable all footrailers to see the bird in the cage. It held capacity crowds at all times. Facing away from the bar, swinging in a semicircle, first came the hors d'oeuvres table—about two Pullman cars long, separated in the middle by the bird. Directly across from the bar, quarter horse distance, was a not-too-hastily constructed replica of an old mining town. Walt Disney himself couldn't have planned it better—the general store, hotel, bank, sheriff's office, saloon, Harry's Holstein and milkmaid, the blacksmith shop, and the barbershop.

In front of the blacksmith shop, Harry's right-hand man, former lumberman and blacksmith, John Rego, shoed a horse, to the wonderment of all. John really was happier shoeing horses than handling his regular job of answering all of Harry's correspondence, but the pay was so good.

On the rail just outside the barbershop, the world's greatest barbershop quarter sang Harry's favorite song:

> "Shoeshine boy in Tacoma
> Cabin boy to Alaska by boat
> Panning gold 'till the northern lights flicker
> Three years never fattened his poke
> That man Harry
> True, fearless, and bold
> Living his life as everyone should
> Fighting for better, better than good."

The quartet had now been singing for exactly one hour. They had started with the cocktail hour at 5 and they would

Business Is Baloney

continue on until 7. At 7, precisely, the lights would go out, signaling the end of cocktails. In that time, the quartet would have sung "Shoeshine Boy in Tacoma," the story of Harry's life, forty times. A brief time out would be called from 7 to 8:30. At 8:30 Harry would make his opening address. At 8:40, his address over, Harry would come down from the stage and lead all of his 1,200 salesmen and their wives to the banquet. That was the plan. Meanwhile back at the ranch…

In front of the Sheriff's office, sitting on the prettiest quarter horse you ever did see, was Tom Ribbon—former heavyweight champion of the world. Tom at one time served as Chief of Police, during the days of the notorious Dillinger. Now he served in the dual capacity of Sheriff of Ramsey County and bodyguard for Harry. Near Tom stood Les Hagen, treasurer of Harry's company, Hall & Hall. Two pearl handled 45's hung low on his 6 foot 3 frame. Les wasn't the fastest gun in the world. Most of his boyhood on an Iowa farm was taken up by plowing 80 acres of rich corn land and shooting squirrels with a 22. In the summer of '39 he came up to the cities and stayed. Harry boosted him from bookkeeper to accountant, to credit manager, to comptroller, and then to vice-president in charge of finance over a period of twenty years. Harry liked Les and believed him to be honest. And Harry liked the idea of an Iowa farm boy pulling himself up by his bootstraps to the top of the ladder. Les himself never appeared to savor the job—really have his heart in it. It didn't really matter, though, because Harry liked him. So, as they moved on, Les, in his fashion, moved with them. Occasionally, he would draw his 45's, raise them high in the air, and explode both at once, shattering the not too acoustically constructed auditorium like a cannon's roar. Then he would smile like Gary Cooper, slip the guns back in their holsters, tilt back his rented 10 gallon hat, and smile some more.

Stump Harrigan, Harry's lobby man, carried his 45's high up on his beer-belly waist. He never fired them. Instead, he preferred to pin the cigarette girls to the porch poles by the General Stores. Whispering sweet nothings into their ears,

Leo T. McCall

promising them everything, expecting to give them nothing, he was made to order to fit perfectly the role of Harry's lobbyist in Washington, D.C. He could pin senators, too, and Harry paid him handsomely for it. Steve could be found at any time, anywhere, making much ado about nothing. What results he ever obtained, only Harry knew. But Harry liked him and that's all that really mattered.

But the center of all attention took place in front of the saloon. There, Harry's wife, Nellie, stylish, 60ish, handsome and confident, stood at a 14 table (not her first one but her first one in some time) shaking dice with seven sales vice-presidents.

Watching over the melee at the hotel entrance stood Harold Hammond. His duties were simple: just make sure that Les Hagen didn't run out of shells; that John Rego didn't run out of nails; and that Harry's wife didn't run out of vice-presidents.

Harry had found Harold running a second-rate hotel in Hot Springs in the early '30's and hired him as a valet of sorts. And Harold could handle the job. Not only did he fulfill all the duties assigned to him but he kept a watchful and apprehensive eye on the Sheriff's quarter horse as well. Harry liked Harold.

This all took place in the lower auditorium. Upstairs in the arena, 45 barbecue pits had been built for broiling steaks. Surrounding the barbecue pits were enough tables for 2,400 guests. Once the broiling began, smoke naturally could be a problem. Russ Fender, number one sales vice-president at the time, was in charge of the barbecuing. He was a salesman's salesman. A tough handshaker, ever ready with a cheese smile, he made everyone feel big and important. He rose to his $50,000 a year job the hard way—no relatives—just long hours of enthusiastic work. Russ was the first to admit he wasn't the smartest guy in the world and his wife was second to agree. Russ visualized no smoke problem whatsoever at all and assured a somewhat skeptical Harry that there wouldn't be any. The steaks came right off Harry's ranch in western Montana. Real choice, top-grade, succulent stuff they were and, in fact, they had to be because they belonged to Harry.

In the theater section adjoining the arena, frantic last-minute alterations were being made to correct the program that had taken six months to rehearse. Here, at 8:30, Harry was to put in his first appearance. And it had to be something no one would ever forget. The Broadway producer, Orian Wakefield himself, had spent a week on Harry's entrance alone. Someone claimed the stage was as large as Radio City Music Hall. But it wasn't—not quite. Wakefield stood, arms akimbo, in the orchestra pit. Overhead a giant crystal ball embedded with thousands of tiny mirrors turned slowly. Wakefield aimed four footlights right at it. Here soon was to be the big moment. At Wakefield's signal, a 22 piece orchestra would play "The Gang's All Here." The giant crystal ball's revolutions would be increased to 60 per minute. All lights would go off except the four floodlights on the spinning ball. Wakefield considered thunder and lightning, which would make the end of the world seem actually anti-climatic. Wakefield himself was to lead the community singing. On cue the orchestra was to cut the music, the crystal ball would fold up into a trap door overhead, and eight floodlights were to be aimed center stage. Here the curtain was to part, revealing a twenty foot full faced photo of Harry, himself, framed by his giant diamond. This touch, Wakefield assured Harry, would bring down the house in thunderous applause. Wakefield thought five minutes would be enough time for applause but Harry told him:

"Let 'em go as long as they want to."

Wakefield questioned whether that would be in good taste. Harry then said:

"Who the hell is running this show?"

Wakefield thought he was. Harry suggested that he take another look into his large crystal ball, at which time Wakefield agreed to let them applaud as long as they wanted to.

Leo T. McCall

After the applause died away, the 22 piece orchestra would play Harry's song "that Man Harry" followed by "You Gotta Have Heart" and "For he's a Jolly Good Fellow." On that cue, Harry's head would be lifted into the wings and Harry, himself, would step out onto the stage. Harry deserved any applause he would be getting. From 2 million in sales in '33 he had built Hall & Hall into 60 million in 1960. 1,200 salesmen sold Hall & Hall's glue in the U.S., Cuba, Mexico, South America, and Canada. Harry's proud statement that his glue stuck to anything, anywhere in the world, was true. The 60 million in '60, however, wasn't all glue. It included the sales of all the subsidiaries of Hall & Hall who made such incidentals as boxes, ink for printing labels, plus four small companies who made products akin to glue, such as tape, ribbon, and oddly enough, paint.

Harry Hall believed in complete sales coverage. When a salesman produced $100,000 in sales and made $20,000 a year, he needed a junior salesman in his territory to help him. Soon the junior salesman, working in the same territory, would have sales of $50,000 a year and the senior salesman's sales would drop to $75,000. The junior salesman (now senior salesman) would soon have a junior salesman, too.

It was thought by those closest to Hall & Hall that a great deal—in fact, most of the applause for Harry—would be coming from all the junior salesmen and their wives.

At 6:45 John Rego carelessly pounded a nail into the sensitive part of a quarter horse's hoof and was promptly kicked into the arms of the barbershop quartet. Les Hagen, somewhat startled by the commotion, fired his two 45's too hastily, burning severely the lovely right arm of his charming wife. Someone later said she clobbered him with her left while getting into the ambulance. But the cocktail party had been in progress for almost two hours by that time, so you couldn't honestly rely on what anybody said.

Rego's blacksmithing job came to an abrupt halt—fifteen minutes ahead of time—as it took four bartenders working over him feverishly to force air back into his lungs. Rego began to revive. Harold Hammond prematurely blinked the lights off and on, indicating the end of the cocktail hour. Rego again passed out, this time in fright.

Tom Ribbon, in the confusion, accidentally spurred his quarter horse. In the blinking darkness and panic that ensued, the quarter horse bounded beneath the bird in the gilded cage. Ribbon took a back somersault off the horse as if he had been decapitated.

By 7:30 the debris had been cleared. Ribbon, luckily, had completed his somersault and landed on his seat. Badly bruised, but not seriously hurt, he managed to regain his composure and collared Hammond, forcing him to leave the lights on.

Hammond lost the key to the door of the cage. However, by 8 o'clock, the Fire Department had sawed through several bars, freeing the imported Italian model. Stump Harrigan calmed Harry's wife, Nellie, as best he could. Then Harry himself arrived at 8:15, at the theater section of the auditorium. No one, outside of Les Hagan's wife, who was in the hospital, was the worse for wear.

So, at 8:30 as pre-arranged, Orian Wakefield raised his baton, signaling the 22 piece orchestra to being "The Gang's All Here." The giant mirrored ball began to revolve at 60 spins a minute. Wakefield led the community sing. As scheduled, the orchestra cut the music, the ball was pulled into the trap door overhead, and the eight floodlights bore down on the twenty foot full-face photo of Harry himself. As anticipated, the applause was thunderous and lasted not five minutes, but fifteen. As the applause finally subsided, the 22 orchestra played Harry's song, "That Man Harry" and, as scheduled, followed with "You Gotta Have Heart" and "For he's a Jolly Good Fellow." Harry's head was then lifted into the wings and Harry, himself, stepped out onto the stage.

He was attired in his usual workday garb. A ten gallon hat tipped jauntily to one side covered his deep Arizona tan. High-

Leo T. McCall

heeled cowboy boots lifted him from 5 feet 10 to 6 foot 1. A Blue silk shirt symbolized that he came to work and not to play. But an imported cream colored coat meant also it was a festive occasion. So he began to talk.

"My whole life is dedicated to this business. My wife comes second. You can ask her. I'm married to this business. I spend every waking hour thinking, planning, and working for you and your families."

"This celebration ain't for me. It's for you. I want a 100 million dollar Hall & Hall and I'm sure you do, too. To achieve it, you must become married to your business like I am. You gotta think of it every minute of every hour like I do. I took this business when it was a two million dollar a year organization and I built it into a sixty million dollar business as it is today. On my shoulders rests the responsibility of all of you. You guys got good jobs. It's up to me to see that you get better ones."

Don't double-cross me. Don't stab me in the back." Harry, his wife smiling proudly beside him, stomped off the steps and waded boldly into the eager and not so eager out-stretched hands of 1,100 salesmen and their wives. His quick, swaggering step, his barrel chested physique, his confident smile—all fitted together to form a picture of a self-made, up from the bottom, "formed under fire," successful executive. But his cold, dead-fish handshake denied it all.

Harry (of course) no longer shined his shoes, cut his own fingernails, shampooed his bald pate, nor drove his own cream colored, leather cushioned Cadillac. His personal chauffeur, his personal butler and his personal (personable) manicurist performed nobly these menial tasks and lived handsomely off the pay.

The somewhat more difficult job of writing his letters and remembering names always was beyond Harry's innate talents. John Rego was paid even more handsomely for this.

Business Is Baloney

As Harry threaded his way through the crowd, John Rego breathed heavily over his shoulder, whispering at every handshake:

"This is Mr. and Mrs. Earnest Starr, Cleveland manager."

"This is Mr. and Mrs. Karl Madden, executive club, Houston."

"This is Mr. and Mrs. Ralph Baker, star salesman, Oakland."

"This is Mr. and Mrs. George Roe, terrific newcomer out of Kansas City."

Harry, on cue, genially greeted each man with a warm, "Hi, ya, Ernie, glad to have you aboard."

Or, "Hi, ya, Karl, I see your ship coming in."

"Remember Karl, keep paddling."

"Take care Ralph, I'm still captain of the ship."

"Nice going George. Stick with me and we'll get through those troubled waters. I'm still on the bridge of the ship.

For variety, Harry would switch from captain of the ship, to top hand at the ranch. His pitch differed somewhat.

"Hi, ya, Bill. Glad to see you back in the saddle."

"Hi, ya, Jim. You sure are corralling those Seattle sales."

"Remember Andy. If you have any trouble breaking those Denver colts, call me."

"Don't worry, Don. I'm still top kick and you can bet I'll die with my boots on."

It was hard for Harry to conceive what went through the minds of the "Hands he had ridden too hard, too long." They met his smiling face with their smiling faces. Some had been given two and three chances (by Harry) to remain on the crew. Still some could have bitten the hand that had fed them or they thought had fed them.

Leo T. McCall

After 500 shakes, Harry, unwittingly garbled his pitch. Things started to come out like, "Hi, ya, Jim. Good to see you ride that bronco through troubled seas."

Or, "Great going George. That's the way to stay aboard that Miami ship and rustle up the herd."

But nobody seemed to mind. In fact, they probably hadn't heard. Long months of planning had resulted in the precision timing of every event.

All chartered airplanes that had carried guests from every major city in the United States had arrived on time. Clear ceilings across the continent was typical of Harry's luck. Had bad weather grounded but on section of the country, many might have missed the only event of its kind in the world.

Points of origin for all flights were centered in seven key spots: Boston, New York City, Philadelphia, Atlantic, Chicago, St. Louis and Los Angeles. Each city housed a home office for Hall & Hall's seven divisions.

Scheduled air lines coming into the celebration city had been cancelled two months previously. This allowed Harry's "Flying Armada" to hit a runway at 60 second intervals. Red carpet treatment at the Terminal was standard procedure—with red carpets for the feet, flowers (flown in from Hawaii) for the ladies, and the band from a local high school blaring away to the excited pleasure of all.

But the big moment had arrived. Harry finished shaking the last hand. He now proceeded to the general arena for the official opening on the banquet and the dance to follow. Several Vice-Presidents attempted to intercept his entrance. But Harry was not to be denied. In typical fashion be brushed aside (and unfortunately therefore didn't hear) their warnings. Evidently something had gone amiss. The smoke from the barbecue pits didn't rise to the ceilings on schedule. Instead it began to choke the guests who were already seated. Water became a necessity.

The big moment had arrived. But the arena was so full of barbecue fumes that you actually couldn't see Harry for the smoke.

Leo T. McCall

Dictionary meaning of
The Boss

"To order about in an arrogant manner"
"A person who makes decisions"
"Exercises authority—dominates"

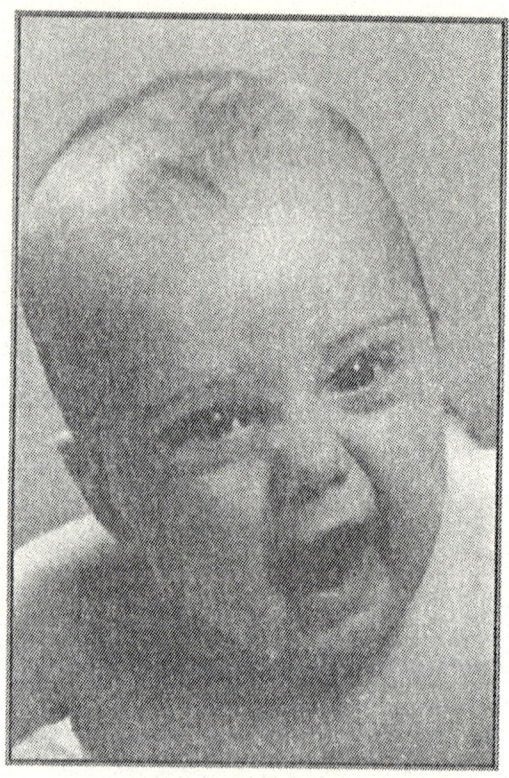

Harry—President—Hall & Hall

[*This caption was placed below the picture in the original.*]

Motto—to get salesmen to sell his product.
"Scare the hell out of them!"

TWO

Wire Reports

Sunday morning, one week after the barbecue, Harry held his first Wire Report meeting. Foxworth's goof was still the subject of conversation. A million dollar party had gone up in smoke!

After the barbecue, the salesmen now had one week of selling time behind them. The barbecue had ended on Sunday. The following Saturday all salesmen were to report their weekly sales volume to their District Managers. Saturday night the District Managers compiled the total sales of their men and wired the results to Hall & Hall so the reports would be in by Sunday morning. Total objective of the first wire: Five Million Dollars!

Sunday morning Wire Reports had become a ritual at Hall & Hall. At 6:30 a.m. precisely, Harry's personal cook arrived. Next to Harry's office, the cook had his own little kitchen...complete with stove, sink, cabinet and liquor (not for Harry, but for his guests).

By 6:40, the coffee was boiling and the grapefruit was cut up. Rumor had it that Harry had the kitchen for breakfast only, as his wife never got up before ten all her life. And Harry felt that breakfast was the most important meal of the day. He had hired a cook, as he put it, "just to keep us alive."

Much had been speculated about Harry and his wife. How could a dynamic man like Harry, devoted as he was to his business, find time to keep a wife happy?

Harry never tried.

Still, his wife worshipped him.

Rumor spread that Harry had a bad heart. The rumor was based on his menu…no starchy foods, plenty of fruit, fish and a maximum of five cups of black coffee a day.

AT 6:50 a.m., Harry's chauffeur, Joe Miller, drove the boss up to the front steps.

Harry had boasted on many occasions that he beat everybody to work in the morning, including the janitor. He drilled into all his help the importance of getting up early—he carried it so far that one year he had a sales promotion campaign entitled: "Early Bird."

In the semi-darkness of the December morning, Harry's silk scarf reflected any available light. Long strides carried him through the electronically controlled doors in the lobby of Hall & Hall. Once inside the lobby, he tightened his imported cowhide belt, adjusted his ten-gallon hat, then skipped up the two flights of stairs to his office.

Once inside, he parted his office curtains and took a long, proud look at the lawn, all covered with snow, and at the sixty-foot evergreen tree already aglow in the cold, clear morning.

"Anybody here?" Harry laughed, knowing the answer.

"A couple of guards," replied the cook.

"Who's picking up the wires?" asked Harry.

"Johnny Rego."

"What time do we start?"

"Same time as usual, Boss. 7:00 a.m.—Sharp!"

"How much do you think we'll do?" asked a very concerned Harry.

"Couldn't say, Boss," answered the cook. "Do you want me to handle the bets again on what the top sales will be?"

"Sure, here's mine." Harry handed him a slip of paper folded once over. On it he had written his guess for the total volume in sales he had expected on the First Wire. Along with his guess, he gave the cook ten dollars…the standard bet.

Business Is Baloney

"Tell Rego I want to see him when he comes in." With that, Harry finished his coffee, spun around and sank into his plush leather chair.

Soon, he was interrupted by the cook, who pushed his head into the room.

"Hey, Boss. Rego's here."

Rego brought the wires in from Western Union at exactly 7:30 a.m. He took them directly to the Director's Room. By now the cook had laid out in the room four boxes of Harry's imported Havana cigars plus three boxes of chocolates plus rolls, doughnuts and two urns of coffee, ham sandwiches and milk. Rego started for the coffee.

Rego's clothes resembled Harry's, but they were toned down considerably in good taste. His ten gallon hat was smaller than Harry's, his cowhide belt a little thinner, his blue shirt a little less blue, his scarf not as silky, and his boots lifted him just one inch, shorter than Harry's.

Now, this was no ordinary Director's Room. It did have a twenty foot oval shaped, mahogany table in the center. But there the resemblance to other big company's Directors Rooms ended.

Branded one inch deep into the center of the table where Harry's initials, H.H.

Everything was branded.

The branded chairs—not really chairs—but western saddles mounted on four legs, encircled the table. A collection of pistols, rifles, lariats, spurs, and photos of Harry astride his many quarter horse chargers covered the four walls.

Harry's own saddle, purposely set up on a pedestal two feet higher than the rest, was made of sterling silver and mounted on four bow legs. The bowlegs were a collector's piece—they came from the piano that had been in the saloon where Jack McCall had shot Wild Bill Hickock.

Harry had wanted swinging doors to the Directors' Room, but at that his wife had balked. The Western theme certainly

Leo T. McCall

needed some limitations and right there it was. It could have "Ride 'Em Cowboy" on a glass panel in the door of the Directors' Room but no, no a thousand times no!...no swinging doors!

Les James sauntered in at 8:00 a.m. and took his usual position at the coffee urn. Painstakingly, he placed his bet on the sales volume for the day and reluctantly parted with ten bucks to the cook.

He would not do much more that morning other than join in on Russ Fender's Victory Cry.

Stump Harrigan arrived at 8:15 a.m. Flamboyantly he placed his bet and joined James. Both Harrigan and James were dressed conservatively in rented Western garb similar to Rego's.

"Good morning, Les," volunteered Stump.

"Ugh," grudgingly retorted Les who never could savor Harrigan.

"What did you guess? Gain or Loss?" asked Stump.

"I'll tell you when they are all posted."

"You won't have to then," reasoned Harrigan. "I'll be able to see it myself."

"That's the idea."

And thus ended Harrigan and James, conversation wise, for the day.

Tom Ribbon hustled in next at 8:20 a.m. followed by the credit manager, comptroller, factory supervisor, top accountant, and special sales executive...all armed with adding machines.

In two minutes they had set up their machines and readied themselves for the 8:30 kick off.

Ribbon grabbed a mitt full of cigars from the box and jammed them in his pocket. He then passed out the tally sheets. All told he passed out sixty sheets, each sheet representing a Hall & Hall District Office. On each sheet, there was listed the previous sales records by man by district.

Business Is Baloney

By 8:30 p.m. all home office Vice-Presidents of Hall & Hall and all promotion men required to keep score had taken their positions. The saddle seats were filled to capacity.

Twenty-five bets had now been placed with the cook for a total payoff of two hundred and fifty dollars.

Russ Fender had called in his bet since he couldn't get in by eight-thirty. He was detained while his wife wrapped Harry's birthday present.

The cook posted the betting at eight-thirty one. The top personnel had bet on the sales volume to be as follows:

HARRY HALL	$5,100,000.00
RUSS FENDER	5,075,000.00
JOHNNY REGO	5,073,125.00
STUMP HARRIGAN	5,000,145.00
LES JAMES	5,000,000.00
TOM RIBBON	4,987,654.00
CHARLIE FOXWORTH	4,980,000.00
THE COOK	4,556,875.00

John Rego walked into the Director's Room with arms held high above his head at 8:35. This signaled the approach of Harry Hall. All personnel jumped from their saddles. Harry entered the room.

In unison all sang:

> Happy Birthday to you,
> Happy Birthday to you,
> Happy Birthday, dear Harry,
> Happy Birthday to you.

Leo T. McCall

Harry Hall, visibly moved, hushed them all with a wave of his hand.

"Thank you, men." Harry blinked his eyes to hold back the tears. "But we have far more important matters to attend to than my birthday."

At this point he jumped into his sterling silver saddle, spurred the piano legs and cried, "Let's round up those five million in sales!"

And everybody jumped into their saddles too.

Right here was Rego's greatest moment. He enjoyed it.

Holding the wire reports high and waving them in the breeze he began to call out sales numbers city by city...

"Atlanta! - $4,000; Dallas! - $5,000; Boston! - $5,500; Seattle! - $3,000; Denver! - $2,500."

As each city was called out, the man assigned to that city rushed to Rego and grabbed the wire report.

Teamwork meant everything.

Recording began the moment the last city of the sixty offices was given out by Rego.

Cities were grouped by seven divisions in Hall & Hall. Each division had a Vice-President. Wire reports ultimately showed what division led in the sales parade.

A likely successor to Harry could come from one of the V.P.'s in charge of a division. Although Harry felt you had to be a successful salesman (as were all of the V.P.'s) to run a business like Hall & Hall—he had never taken as much as one order himself. So, on the contrary, most V.P.'s thought that the likely successor would be Rego, Foxworth, James, Harrigan, Fender or Wakefield.

But most inside men like Rego and Harrigan were frustrated by their lack of "Firing line field experience" and, logically, looked to the V.P.'s for their new leadership, even though to run a company you didn't need to know how to sell.

"You had to run the men who run the sales force," Fender would say many years after Harry had passed away. "And Harry ran the men around him and he ran them ragged."

Two inside men would take the wires in from Milwaukee and, armed with last year's figures, would run the new total. One read the figures—the other recorded them. Finished with Milwaukee, they would have a total comparison:

MILWAUKEE OFFICE SALES

PAST YEAR	NEW FIGURE
$7,800	$7,000

Milwaukee sales then would pass on the accountants for verification. Audited and corrected (when necessary) they would then pass on to each assigned leader for that division. The assigned leader then would run to Harry and cry:

"Milwaukee...Northern Division! Loss: $800.00."

Charlie Foxworth, sitting next to Harry, had his own tabulating sheet listing each District office...by division with the number one office from the previous year on top followed by the next line.

Foxworth would then advise Harry as to the leader of each District and the leader of all the Districts.

The leader of each Division would have a personal call from Harry that day. The leader of all Divisions would not only get a personal telephone call but a dozen roses from Harry himself for his wife.

On the advice of Russ Fender, Harry had spent a million dollars on the Jubilee.

Fender assured Harry that nothing but good could come from the Jubilee and Harry had believed him.

This could be Fender's mistake—not Harry's.

Leo T. McCall

"Harry," said Fender, "I'll bet a million dollars you'll get a ten million dollar gain after the Jubilee!"

In twenty to twenty-five minutes the results would be known.

Rego sensed trouble when one of the key cities in the U.S., Indianapolis, showed a three thousand dollar loss.

Harry stiffened in his saddle when he heard it but showed no other emotion. Rego tried to hurry over the loss in Chicago of nine grand but Harry couldn't help but hear it when Foxworth yelled it in his ear.

Halfway through the tabulation, Russ Fender presented Harry his birthday gift, a picture of a new Cadillac. It didn't help. Everything indicated that sales were going down the Hall was in for a tough time.

Harry rode uneasily in the saddle. Even his present, a bulletproof Cadillac, with shatterproof windows and holstered forty-fives on the inside of each door, failed to divert his unease.

As Vice President of Sales, Russ Fender could con Harry or anyone with whom he came in contact, but who could con a thousand salesmen into selling if competitors outnumbered them.

"Fender!" roared Harry.

"Yes Sir!" a comin' running Fender said.

"Fender, I thank you for the Caddy."

"You are welcome, Sir," said Fender.

"I'll tell you this, though, Fender," said Harry, changing the subject. "They'll never catch Old Paint off guard with this fancy rig. He'll still know I'm going to let him ride free."

All this referred to Harry's favorite quarter horse...Old Paint.

"We didn't want you to catch Old Paint in this Caddy, Sir. We just wanted you to enjoy your ride to work in the morning."

Business Is Baloney

Each V.P. and each District Manager was assessed in proportion to their salary for the annual gift...whether they wanted to or not...

Harry's wife usually selected the gift.

"He can't catch Old Paint anymore, Russ. Maybe with the Caddy he can."

The amount of Caddy collection was short by five thousand. And Fender gladly threw in the difference...just that amount would replace his contribution to the Red Cross.

Fender concluded his presentation speech, "This will be Hall & Hall's greatest year. I have every confidence it will be. I tell you, Harry, every man in this room feels as I do. We're shooting fish in the barrel. We're hitting the sitting ducks. We've got the sugar in the bin."

Then Fender waxed eloquently.

"Gentlemen. You know who built this business. You know who took us through our troubles. Harry pointed our way to the smoky smokestacks, to the ducks in the pond when we couldn't see the forest for the trees."

References to the ducks in the pond, sugar in the bin, and fish in the barrel all had a personal meaning to Harry. These were all expressions of his greatest sales manager, himself.

Fender continued, "Follow the river and you shall come to sea. Follow the dollars and you'll come home to me."

This broke Harry's last wall of resistance.

He dismounted from the sterling silver saddle and put his head on Fender's shoulder tearfully.

Harry raised Fender's arm high over both their shoulders.

Fender jumped to the top of the mahogany table. Completely broken up by his own speech he did what only he could have thought of doing to bring everyone back to their senses...he gave the Fender victory cry:

"Da…da…da…da…da…da…da…da…da…da…da…da…da…da…da…da…da…BOOM DE AYE."

Standing on the top of the HH brand and to the tune of Sousa's Stars and Stripes Forever, he made a magnificent picture.

Then in unison all men present jumped to their saddles and echoed:

"BOOM DE AYE."

In honor of the Southern salesmen, the District Manager of Atlanta added:

"YOU ALL."

The final figures were not in on all divisions. They showed a slight loss over the previous year. That was not good. Hall & Hall had not shown a loss in five years. Harry Hall didn't like it.

Harry had just spent one million dollars. Harry had been assured of a gain by Fender. Harry was not getting his gain. Fender was on the chopping block!

Final figures came to a total of $4,450,000.00! The cook had won the bets.

But the gift of the Caddy, the spirit of the men around him and Fender's tremendous enthusiasm and unbounding confidence that all would be well at Hall & Hall kept all spirits high. And Harry, taken away by the enthusiasm led the tidal wave joy with a Victory Cry himself:

"Da…da…da…da…da…da…da…da…da…da…da…da…da…da…da…da…da…. BOOM DE AYE."

The only calm person left in the group on the Sunday morning sales rally was the cook. And he was busy counting the $250.00 he had just won.

THREE

Miami Bound

On the following morning, after the wires were in and the situation appeared bleak, Harry began an ill-fated week.

Of the few offices showing gains, the Miami District led by a tremendous gain. Typical of the man of action that he was, Harry headed for Miami.

How come Miami could run with the ball so fast and score touchdowns? Harry had to know.

He left his wife behind.

Harry, in his own good time, dated a few girls. The office help under Rego's guidance took bets on which girl Harry would marry.

Many bet on the receptionist—a real beauty with a dazzling smile and Hollywood figure. Others bet on the telephone operator—a sultry voice and 'come up and see me some time' invitation.

But the winner (Rego's choice) was the manager of Napoleon's Cafe across the street from the main plant. Harry fell in love with her bossy management style and strawberry blond looks.

Miami lured Harry. He liked the beach, the swampland, the ocean fishing, the dog races, the hotels and motels, the excitement of the Miami nights. To go and see the Miami office in the front-running served a double purpose. He had to go to determine what pattern of sales the Miami manager was using to increase his sales in the face of a decline throughout the country. Secondly, he liked to go to enjoy what lured him.

Leo T. McCall

Once he found the pattern of success used by the Miami manager, he could show that pattern to the rest of his managers and immediately avert what appeared to be a downward trend in business.

In most businesses, sales managers are hired for that particular job.

Why Fender was obviously not going reflected the downward plunge in business. Fender had not been able to manipulate gain. After the wire reports, Harry and his cook headed for the railroad depot to get the next train to Miami.

At the railroad depot, the Hall & Hall high school band (pre-arranged by Rego) blared away in school boyish dissonance. At 10:30 p.m. they had wearied a little but to stay out past the high school curfew was an occasion itself.

Harry's departure at 11:00 p.m. for Chicago was not a major event itself, but the leader of the band, as Christmas neared, took, grasped, or opportunely instigated a need to give Harry a rousing farewell. To the bandleader this could mean an attractive bonus.

Harry entered the train. The band played endlessly. Pullman car passengers, long since retired, were unimpressed.

Foxie arrived in time to tap the bandleader gently on the shoulder. The leader swung around as if he had been hit by a rubber bindered staple. He recovered quickly and smiled.

Foxie shouted in his ear, "Stop the music!"

At this cue the leader blew the whistle. The music stopped in a few jerks.

"Play Alabama bound," screamed Foxie (Harry's short-cut name for Foxworth).

"He's going to Florida," blasted back the bandleader.

"Do you know Florida bound?"

That was enough for the leader. He played Alabama Bound. Harry waived his ten gallon hat for a minute. He took his hand

Business Is Baloney

off the rail of the car. As the car started suddenly, Harry fell off the train.

He recovered quickly, jumped back on the now moving train and without so much as a look back climbed up the steps and disappeared into the train.

Foxie had arranged the train tickets, since Harry refused to fly in an airplane, even since the company plane once overshot the Kansas City runway and ditched into the Missouri River.

Fortunately, no one had been injured.

The pilot, who had flown many combat missions in World War II without mishap, insisted he hadn't been at the controls. Many suspected that Harry had been.

The pilot was suspended indefinitely but later turned up as one of Hall & Hall's topnotch salesmen working out of Atlanta, Georgia.

Foxie, on stern orders from Harry, always tipped the porters heavily. And Harry's name had by now become synonymous with good tipper on the Milwaukee Road.

Foxie carried the lunch basket especially prepared by Harry's cook...not his wife. It contained a few snacks for midnight enjoyment—rye krisp, apples, peaches for Harry and Coca Cola for Foxworth. Some train passengers looked suspiciously at the basket. Harry was well known.

A man of obvious means need not have to travel carrying his own lunch!

On one occasion Harry had insisted on inspecting the dining car kitchen personally. On being refused with some nonsensical remark by the conductor that it was against the Milwaukee Road's policy, Harry was heard to say:

"Listen road man. As long as I live I will never eat another meal on your bankrupt road!"

And to the day he died he didn't.

Harry's knowledge of train schedules in his own time was legendary. He knew the midnight special would arrive in Chicago at seven forty-five in the morning. He knew that the nine forty-five City of Miami would leave Chicago on time to reach Miami at five forty the next afternoon.

And he knew all the schedules and all the connections for every city in the United States, whether the trains were going to Miami, New Orleans, Boston, Seattle or Butte.

So how he and Foxie were deposited at the Milwaukee depot instead of the Chicago Union Station at five in the morning only the heavily tipped porters would ever know.

Harry never drank and neither did Foxie. Evidently the heavily tipped porters must have heavily imbibed.

"Chicago!"

"Chicago!"

Off the train when Harry and Foxie.

With Foxie driving Hall & Hall's Milwaukee Manager's car and Harry guiding them with a road map, the two arrived in Chicago with a good half hour to spare before the City of Miami left for Florida.

The lunch had been left on the train. Knawing hunger pangs forced Foxie and Harry to grab a quick snack at the Illinois Central restaurant. Harry's three minute egg took two minutes too long to prepare. Since the egg was too hard to swallow, he switched to Cream of Wheat. Lumps in the Cream of Wheat choked him up so badly that he fell into a coughing spell.

Right then and there he refused to pay the bill.

Harry screamed at the cashier: "Your eggs are too hard. Your Cream of Wheat is too lumpy. Your toast is too cold. Your service is non-existent. Call the manager. I insist your cook be fired!"

With that, he bolted out of the depot.

Business Is Baloney

The rest of the day passed uneventfully. But the night did not.

Because of the nearness of the Holiday season Foxie had had trouble getting a compartment on the train to Miami and had to settle for a side-by-side roomette with Harry.

Luggage normally could be kept in compartments at either end of the Pullman.

Common sense dictated more caution that to foolishly leave the heavily engraved, genuine cowhide luggage of Harry's wife open to stealing.

Harry insisted on taking all the luggage, including Foxie's cardboard cartons, into their roomettes. Three porters, Foxie, and Harry forced the luggage into the two roomettes.

When Harry and Foxie finally settled down their doors were blockaded by suitcases.

At one in the morning a buzzer brought Harry to a sitting position in his bed.

"Who's there?"

No answer.

Harry drifted back into the semi-sleep only possible on a train.

After the buzzer. This time Harry got up—removed all the suitcases in front of his door and peeked outside.

No one was there.

He went back in—piled all the suitcases in front of the door again—drifted again into the semi-sleep, but with a cocked ear.

By two thirty the buzzer had awakened Harry three times and one three occasions Harry had removed all the luggage to answer.

Six in the morning found him fully dressed sitting in his dining car.

Leo T. McCall

Falling off the train, being left off at Milwaukee, going without breakfast, and being kept awake all night was nothing compared to what happened to Harry in Miami the next day.

The Miami police accused him of murdering his District Manager, John Reardon.

The following day he was exonerated. Foxie thought it was funny, but Harry didn't.

The case was unusual.

The judge asked "Mr. Hall, please tell the court in your own words exactly what happened when you and Mr. Reardon went fishing?" So Harry told him this story.

"I asked John to join me in a private fishing trip. I wanted to go somewhere where we could talk in private. He took me to a little lake home up in the lowlands. For four hours from six in the morning to ten we trolled.

"I knew it took a long time for John to loosen up before he'd tell me how he had sales gains going. Personally, I didn't care about fishing...in fact four hours without a bite can be boring. The boiling sun did not lend itself to the great hope that fish actually were in the lake.

'Are you sure you wouldn't rather be eating a snack?' asked John. He shut off the two-horsepower motor for a short rest and put some live bait on his hook.

'No sir,' I replied. 'This is the life for me. Anyway I had a big breakfast.'

"John then started the motor again and off we went. I tried to take the motor for a while but he wouldn't let me."

'Just keep your line away from the propeller and we'll get along just fine,' he retorted.

"I reminded him that I had got my line caught in the motor only once in four hours which wasn't too bad. In fact, it was the only excitement we had."

"I thought I had a whale for the tremendous pull it gave. The rod bent at right angles. The reel spun like a top. It took twenty minutes to untangle it.

"The wind now came up and I'd say was blowing fifteen to twenty miles an hour. Here and there weeds could be seen as we drifted closer to shore.

"Water near shore was shallow...six to eight feet deep.

"Instead of loosening John up as I intended, he just kept getting more upset.

"I finally persuaded him to let me run the motor so he could concentrate on trolling.

"To this he agreed.

"In five minutes he had not caught a thing.

"Then all hell broke loose.

"A fish hit my line!"

(At this point in the testimony, Harry was most exacting and tried to give as clear a picture of the accident as he could.)

"I was in the back of the boat trolling to my right. John was in front trolling to my left...facing me it was to his right.

'What'll I do?' I cried to John.

'Reel him in,' he screamed.

'What about the motor?'

'Cut it off,' he yelled...much louder than before.

"I cut the motor off and started to reel. Now keep in mind, your Honor, I was bringing this thing in to my right. It was big enough for a net and the net lay at the bottom of the boat.

"In his haste to get the net, John threw his line over my head. I ducked. Now remember, your Honor, both lines are now on the same side of the boat.

"He grabbed the net. He held his line. His left hand and his right jammed the net in the water. In an attempt to grab the fish and bring it into the board, he broke the line.

"The fish escaped."

The following part of the testimony was hard to believe. But Harry told it so often and each time the same that the judge, the police and the people believed it to be true.

"The fish became entangled in John's line and his line encircled the fish's fin. This caught John by complete surprise and he was catapulted into the water. The fish bolted high in the air three times. It weighted forty to forty-five pounds. John refused to let go of the line. He was dragged ten to eleven yards in the water by the fish. I never saw John again," testified Harry.

Late the next afternoon, John's body was dragged out of the water.

The fish, with the line encircled around his fin was never found.

Harry stayed over for the funeral.

He left Miami in an ugly mood.

He never found out the secret of John's success and he never again found an adequate replacement.

Harry thought the downward plunge in business could not be stopped.

FOUR

Montana Mission

"Go to the mountains."
"Breathe in the mountain air."
"Sit in solitude amidst the splendor of the Rockies."
"Fish for trout."
"Commune with nature."
"Think deep thoughts."
"Shoot moose."
"Play poker with friends."
"Get lost."

This sound advice came from Harry's wife who often told him with wifely concern that his troubled thoughts were too deep for her.

On Monday after his return from Miami, Harry called an emergency meeting of his "spirit and morale" staff.

Monday night the staff flew to Moose Lodge just east of the Rockies in Northern Montana. Since Kansas City Harry had never flown again. Charlie and Harry took the train.

It was now obvious.

The first wire report had been padded!

Sales had dropped even greater than the wire reports had shown. Final tabulations of the incoming orders clearly showed business to be $4,250,000.00 and not $4,460,000.00!

Ironically, Miami showed a loss.

Rego could be counted on to keep Harry's morale up.

Leo T. McCall

He knew how: Feed Harry's ego.

Tell Harry he still was the greatest leader in the world. Tell Harry his men had betrayed him. Tell Harry the world's against him. Tell him anything. But don't tell Harry he might have made a few mistakes himself.

After one hour with Rego, Harry would be so livid and uncontrollable that he would then drive his men beyond the limits of their own endurance—with the end result...a chain reaction of fear would spread from the bottom of the organization to the top and each man in his turn would work his head off for fear of displeasing the boss and losing his job.

The "morale squad" consisted of the inner circle—John Rego, Russ Fender, Stump Harrigan, Charles Foxworth and of course Harry himself.

Rego, Fender and Harrigan had spent most of Monday night in a hotel in Butte.

Rego had bunked down with Shakespeare's *Hamlet* and had worried himself to sleep.

Fender and Harrigan had drifted to the Bonga Bar.

Rego claimed the next morning he heard shots during the night. But then he also claimed a scorpion interrupted his reading by running back and forth across his chest during his reading time.

It was common knowledge that Fender always carried a loaded gun.

Fender was not a big man, so he carried the gun for protection. For years he had traveled thousands of miles over his division, which represented a third of the United States.

The gun did not give him extra confidence. He had enough of that. Very simply, the reason for the 38 was that no one was going to rob him of his money without getting into a life and death struggle. Fender just played it that way.

Business Is Baloney

In fight circles, Fender would be classified as a counter puncher.

Harry had found him in a gas station pumping gas and good will for twenty five bucks a week.

Harry put him on the road selling glue.

"If you can peddle gas, young man, you can peddle glue," Harry insisted.

Fender proved he could peddle glue. During his first year in the business he peddled eight thousand dollars worth of glue.

Slowly he rose in the company and eventually he became a vice president. Twenty five years it took him—and the hard way.

Except for a new Cadillac each year and a diamond stick pin or two, Fender had few needs.

So why drive so hard so long?

He didn't drive. He just counteracted.

A million light jabs won't knock you out but they will make you a little sensitive after a while.

During Fender's twenties, It took about ten to fifteen light jabs in the morning to get him ready for the day. Casual remarks from his wife did it.

"Shut the cupboard door."

"Hang up your pajamas."

"Please get the meat for supper."

"Gas up the car."

"Feed the baby."

"Dump the garbage."

"Pay the milkman."

"Shovel the sidewalk."

"Straighten your tie."

"Ask for a raise."

Leo T. McCall

"I need money."

In the fight for recognition as potential sales manager of such a tremendous firm as Hall & Hall, Fender fought cleanly and openly.

By the time he reached his office each morning he was on his toes, alert, counter punching beautifully, jabbing his District Manager in Toledo, blasting his Star Salesman in Chicago, nailing with vicious rights and lefts any lethargy or laziness on the part of all who worked under him.

As the years passed, each new sales quota became a more difficult obstacle to overcome. If Fender had missed a few it wouldn't have been so bad. But each quota he made—where many others had failed. Bitterness had begun to creep into his system. Now that Hall & Hall was losing sales day after day, the long pace began to take its toll. Fender was now going against his own sales figures—figures he had made the previous year—and the year before that and the year before that. Harry couldn't understand why Fender couldn't at least break even with a year ago. Certainly (as sales manager) Fender had the most knowledge of where the business is and how to get it.

So as Fender stood at the bar with Harrigan (never his friend) and took two shots in quick succession—he loosened up. And here in the Bonga Bar far from home, Harrigan became his confidant, Father Confessor and only friend.

"This mistake, Steve, is not in setting quotas," expostulated Fender, "but in making them."

"I don't follow."

"Have you ever been to the Olympics?"

"No I haven't," puzzled Steve replied. "But what has that to do with the sales quotas?"

"Everything. Take a pole vaulter. Take the broad jumper. Take the high jumper. All have limitations. Right?"

"Right."

Business Is Baloney

"No one can vault 20 feet. Yet. Right?" Not waiting for a confirmation, Fender continued with the cold logic of his argument.

"Anybody leap 30 feet? Who has hit the high jump at 8 feet? No one. Right?"

"I'll take your word for it. No one has vaulted 20 feet, no one has leaped 30 feet and no one has jumped 8 feet. So what?" asked Steve in his usual disinterested tone.

"Because it isn't humanly possible—yet." Fender switched to a cool Coors but Harrigan held to his scotch and soda.

"Fender, I don't follow you," said Steve with finality.

"It's simple," reasoned Fender. "You spend a year training for the Olympics. You aim at the 20 foot pole vault. So from 14' you jump to 15' but you don't make 20'. You don't expect to make 20 but it's a nice goal. Harry expects you to make 20'."

"The impossible?"

"The impossible. There's no harm in trying to 20' and settling for 15' (the best you can do anyway). But to expect 20' is insanity. Harry expects 20'." (Fender was not repeating for emphasis. Whiskey followed by beer had his mind and he said 20' again because he couldn't remember saying it the first time.)

In Fender's bear trap mind the argument was over. In Harrigan's mind it had never begun. He began to create the quota logic as only he could see it.

"You can't criticize Harry." (Steve noticed that the bartender caught a glimpse of Fender's gun.) He must be gun-shy by now.

Politically astute, Steve never mixed the too highly explosive drink of business and pleasure. Patiently he listened to all of Fender's grievances. The fun of living for the moment stopped him from taking Fender seriously. After all, Steve's bread and butter was made in the corridors of Congress not in the Bonga Bar in Butte.

For several minutes during Fender's heavy exposé of sales quotas, he disappeared, ostensibly headed for the door with the gentleman's top hat on it. Fender switched automatically to the bartender during Steve's absence and automatically back to him when he came back.

"And another point," continued Fender, "about making a quota. Say you can jump a 2 foot fence. With practice you leap to 3 feet, then after more practice you hurdle 3 feet. How long can you go on. Forever? Soon the target's on a 10 story building and you can't even reach the awnings. What's Harry thinking of? Who does he think can jump so high. Who?"

Steve returned from the top hat room.

Fender no longer was patting the bar lightly with the palm of his hand to make a point. The counter puncher now was banging each point with clenched fists—shifting to Steve's right then to Steve's left...weaving back and forth beautifully...moving, moving, moving.

After the bar closed at 1 a.m., Steven went directly to his room. Fender hung on until the bartender locked the door and tried to wish Fender a pleasant good night.

Fender held the bartender 10 minutes more. His keen mind had developed another cold logical argument against the making of sales quotas.

"Say, for instance, you jump a two foot creek...then a five foot creek, etc., etc., etc. Soon Harry will have me trying to jump the wide Missouri. And hell, he knows I can't even swim!"

At 1:30 a.m. the bartender broke loose and disappeared into the night. The night clerk (asleep or awake) refused to answer Fender's clang, clang on the desk bell. Fender then reluctantly headed for his room. On Saturday night this could have been the shank of the evening. On Monday night the sidewalks had long been rolled up and put to bed.

Business Is Baloney

Carpeted floors muffled his cleated shoes. The bang and clang of heavy elevator chains came to an abrupt halt as the elevator returned to the ground floor. Fender clumsily opened the door to his room and flicked on the light. He stepped into the room but never got the door shut. At the foot of his bed sat a timber wolf, fangs showing, ready to spring. Fender pulled his 38 and unloaded all six shells into it. It never so much as blinked an eye.

Rego and Harrigan denied ever having seen or heard of Fender when questioned by the police one half hour later. Both retired. Fender was warned by the police not to take such matters into his own hands. As a precaution, however, Fender reloaded his gun and the police could do nothing about it…after all he carried a legitimate permit.

Police ordered the clerk to see that the damaged wolf be taken back to the local taxidermist for repair and restored to his rightful place in the local museum.

Fender peered down from his window just in time to watch the squad car turn the corner and disappear. Then he walked into the bathroom to brush his teeth. When he opened the medicine cabinet he unwittingly released two pigeons. Startled as he was, he kept his presence of mind. Once again he drew his 38 and filled the air with another six rounds of ammunition, shattering the silence of the night like a cannon's roar and practically blowing the pigeons to pieces.

Rego explained Fender's actions to the judge.

"Your Honor, this man is not dangerous! Certainly after these strange events I could not demand his release, but at least I can vindicate his actions. What's the bail?"

The judge (awakened at 2:15 a.m.) cared for neither vindication nor bail.

"Have this man appear in court for disturbing the peace at 10:00 a.m. with proper legal counsel. He'll need it. (Turning to the police officers) "Who authorized calling me at this hour?"

Officer to the judge, "He showed me his police badge (pointing to Fender). He's deputy sheriff of Ramsey County. He demanded justice from a fellow law officer."

On Tuesday night, all three, Rego, Fender, and Harrigan arrived at the Lodge. It was locked. Harry wouldn't arrive until the next night with the key. In a shed out in back Rego uncovered several mountain tents. He took over. He placed the food they had brought from Butte into a three foot hole that he dug. Here it wouldn't freeze. Several sticks and his red handkerchief alerted anyone near it not to step down or else they would land on their stock of potatoes, cartons of milk, bread, eggs, cartons of canned vegetables and meat. He quickly instructed Fender and Harrigan in the tricky business of putting up the tents. Harrigan caught on at once but Fender clumsily erected the tent from the inside and nearly suffocated before he got out.

Fender complained most of the night and especially early in the morning when he fell into the hold holding the food, breaking all the eggs and spraining his right ankle.

"Take your job with Hall & Hall like you would take a wife," Fender could be often quoted, "Love it blindly, give all of yourself and you will be rewarded. Marriage is a mutual affair.

"Each gives and each receives. Blind faith in each other must prevail. Discontent and divorce come from distrust first and then disillusionment. Look at what you are entering—a lifetime partnership. Your job is a marriage of you and the work to be done. Enter it with blind faith. Give all of yourself and rewards will come.

"Your great potential will have arrived. Discontent and disillusionment cannot break the barrier any easier than a glider can break the sound barrier. Together we shall go forward with Harry to a bigger and better society...to the finer things of life...to the greatest business in the world."

Fender would give this speech to each new recruit. In fact, as sales manager of a district office, he once gave the speech to

Business Is Baloney

52 men in a year before it influenced one. But most important of all he believed every word of what he said.

Rego had heard the pitch many times himself. Fender would gladly give it on request any place, anytime, anywhere. At the end would come the Fender Victory Cry.

When Fender dropped into the pit at 4:30 a.m. (in the dead of night) and came out limping and cussing, Rego wondered how the marriage was coming along. He contemplated that the marriage of Fender and the Hall & Hall business certainly could be in jeopardy. Not only was his job on the chopping block because of falling sales but physical discomfort plagued him as did pride and loss of it. Fender bridled under another fact: Rego (his obvious enemy since Rego stood on the right hand side of Harry) had paid his bail in Butte and he was obligated to him.

Fender nursed his ankle. Rego puffed pensively away on his filtered corncob pipe and Harrigan, blissfully unaware of all about him, slept merrily on until dawn.

Harrigan was not the worrying kind. He would rather be embroiled in politics than in business. As in the usual rags to riches story, he had begun by carrying newspapers in the lower middle class section of town. As in the upper, the upper middle, the middle and the lower class sections some people were chiselers, but most were not. He soon learned that the old lady living in the house on the edge of Moose Swamp, gentle and kind to cats, dogs, canaries and parrots, would sooner clip him for the 76 cents a month for the paper than she would beat the biting dog, let the canary get caught by the cat or talk back to the canary.

His rise in politics described by the local paper as phenomenal and unprecedented etc. etc. etc. was nothing of the kind. As a big frog in a small pond he not only croaked all night but all day too. He never took firm stands on controversial issues. Like a rock—righteous, unwavering and resolved he stood out openly against murder and rape.

Leo T. McCall

He became friendly in the presence of little boys and little girls.

Harrigan's first office was in the state legislature. One year prior to his election he set the pattern of his life in politics: get your name in front of the public and keep it there.

At the ball game Harrigan could be found, providing the band was there, beating the drums. At the football game if given half the chance he would grab a baton and strut proudly behind the baton-twirling majorette. In church (denomination differed from week to week) Harrigan could find the first pew but not without much ado. He scanned the death notices before he glimpsed the headlines. Strange indeed was the fact that Harrigan could get into the inner sanctum of both the Knights and the Masons.

No one made a phone call, wrote a letter, stopped him on the street or saw him in his office who later didn't receive a note from him—acknowledging the meeting, the request or the inquiry—whether he ever did anything for him or not...at least they heard from Harrigan. He became a knight in shining armor—a crusader for lost causes.

As an acknowledged leader of the "little men" and defender of big business, Harrigan never introduced a bill in legislature, never served on a committee, and never (when he could avoid it) voted on a controversial issue.

Harrigan could play the piano by ear—a rare talent. At any social gathering, a bridge party, a charity ball, a church social, club meeting; anywhere where a piano was in sight, he would (whether invited or not) sit boldly down and play loudly and rhythmically: HARRIGAN, THAT'S ME!

Here in the cold dawn of northern Montana rested three of the morale squad. Swiftly over the flat, monotonous plains of North Dakota and into the desolate eastern part of Montana came Harry and Foxie for this meeting, from which would come the moment of truth, the future of Hall & Hall. Harrigan's contribution would of course be nothing. Fender, now

Business Is Baloney

completely on the defensive, could be nothing but ineffectual and resentful.

Harry, now in the twilight of his brilliant career, was going through the motions. He was greatly concerned and if necessary would return to the position of general sales manager or as he put it "to the bridge of the ship."

Foxworth, his traveling valet, butler and intimate friend could not be called on to do anything but supply food and entertainment. It appeared that the shrewd and highly capable Rego alone could salvage something from this ill-fated meeting. Rego was once heard to say, definitely not to be quoted, that Harry would have been better off to quit when he was ahead.

Rego's conception of the business was sound. He knew its strengths and weaknesses, its potential for growth and its limitations. Knowing this and knowing also all the divisional vice presidents and their district managers, he could project the possible effect of the meeting and just what it could accomplish. He held little faith in anything coming out of it at all. To him, the whole outcome should be to get Harry interested in something besides business.

Rego awoke first. He had failed to compensate for the one hour time change and when his wrist alarm sounded off at 7:00 a.m., it was really 6:00 a.m. mountain time. He silently cursed Harry for the watch. Since Harry had given it to him, he had no alternative but to wear it. He stuffed tobacco into his pipe, sat up, lit it and looked over at Harrigan and Fender still asleep. The aggregate salary, mused Rego, of all three of them tipped well over a $100 grand.

Rego glanced at Fender, who after a long night of twisting, turning, moaning, mumbling and jerking, had finally fallen asleep. As far as Harry was concerned, Fender was doomed. The problem now was how to eliminate him and justify it. Fender's cheerleader's antics were great while the team was winning but quite obviously it would take more than some stand up cheers to pull Hall & Hall out of the mud.

Leo T. McCall

Harrigan would cloud the issues with big talk of a $100,000,000 Hall & Hall—talk that Harry always liked. But Harrigan was far too cunning to take a bite at the big apple—general sales manager. He would content himself with the big House Accounts, baby them with ever loving care, protect them as though they were his own.

Fender awoke with a start when Rego screamed: "Run for the hills men, the Indians are coming."

Harrigan refused to eat any breakfast without eggs. Rego suggested that he go back into town and buy them which he promptly did. In town he ran into what could have caused a long delay.

Thirty seconds before he entered the supermarket, it had been robbed. Harrigan approached the checkout clerk. She stood paralyzed.

"Where are the eggs?" he demanded. Then he noticed money on the floor...just a few 5's and 20's.

"He wore a stocking...nylon. It covered his face." She mumbled to a woman shopper who also had seen the bandit.

"Where do you keep your chicken eggs?" Harrigan thought they may have misunderstood the question.

The woman shopper said, "Yes he wore a mask...a nylon stocking."

The check out clerk reiterated, "He wore a stocking nylon. It covered his face."

"Do you keep the eggs out by the meat counter?" Harrigan's questions seemed fair enough.

"Yes, he wore a mask, a nylon stocking."

Harrigan moved down one aisle after another. He came to the butcher.

"How are you fixed for a dozen or so eggs?"

The butcher replied, "Besides a stocking that distorted his features, he wore a ten gallon Texas hat."

Business Is Baloney

"I'd like a dozen eggs. I'm hungry."

The butcher never heard him. "He went out the back door. The T.V. repairman called the police."

Harrigan discovered the eggs, picked up two dozen, then asked the butcher the cost.

"Besides a mask that distorted his face, he wore a ten gallon Texas hat" was all the butcher could tell him.

At the checkout counter he ran into the same trouble.

"He wore a stocking...nylon. It covered his face" so mumbled the check out girl. The woman shopper was no help either.

"Yes, he wore a mask—a nylon stocking" was all she could say.

Harrigan picked up three pair of nylon stockings and a five dollar bill off the floor and then attempted to pay. The girl just stood there staring the same as when he came in. Just then the police arrived. They lumbered out of the squad car, made sure that the culprit was safely out of sight (they looked, oh so slowly, up the street and then down) and entered the market for routine questioning.

Harrigan gave the first cop the $5 telling him it was for what he bought. As he left the store he saw the cop pocket the five.

On the way back to the Lodge, Harrigan stopped at the post office and mailed his wife the stockings. It was the least he could do.

Meanwhile back at the Lodge, Rego finished cooking the bacon. And when Harrigan arrived, Fender was attempting to fold his tent.

"Here are the eggs."

All three sat there at the foot of the mountain and ate heartily indeed.

All day the three napped, smoked, walked in the woods, cussed each other out and cursed their fate. None prepared any

Leo T. McCall

constructive suggestions for pulling Hall & Hall from the doldrums.

At 5:00 p.m. they started for the railroad station to meet Harry. At 5:30 p.m. the front right wheel spun off their Hertz Rent-A-Car Chevrolet. Fender went for the long walk—about a mile to the closest house for a phone. To pass time Rego turned on the radio. One station came in good—too good. You could hear it. It was blaring the hit song of the day: "Boogie Man". Rego cringed when the lyrics hit his esthetic sense:

"If you like boogie, woogie, you're a boogie woogie fan. *I* like boogie woogie. Why call *me* boogie man?"

Rego couldn't take anymore. So he clicked it off.

"Harry can accomplish nothing by having this meeting that hasn't been done already. The new line is out. The men are working. Should we have a contest? Why? Why?"

Rego went on and on and on:

"We must divert his attention to something else. Take his mind off the business for a couple months. The peak has been reached. Our competition gets stronger. Small manufacturers with little overhead keep murdering us on prices. Remember, Harrigan, when you're the kind of the hill the forces are mustering together down below."

Rego continued: "Fender's not long for his job. Harry's used him up. Fender knows it. You know it. I know it. Harry will return to the bridge of the ship—take command ostensibly away from Fender, who never had it from the beginning. He'll scan the horizon for new ambitious heads springing up over the wheat. Count he times we've been through this. Names names.

Ivan Dahlich, Harvey McCue, Charlie Walton, Tom Rustad, Dick Bockman, Ernie Bruback, Newell Preston, Walt Nylon, Tom Collins, Otto Stinson, Tom Freeman. Need I go on?"

Business Is Baloney

"You missed the most important one," interjected Harrigan.

"Who is that?"

"Paul Strandberg."

"That's right. Now here's the thing to do. Fender has many friends. Right? Right! Never jump off the horse in the middle of the stream! Save Fender at any cost at least until this year is over. This delaying action can be explained as a period of re-evaluation. Pass the word to refigure the budget at once—thereby saving the profit picture. Realistically speaking this should have been done 5 years ago."

Harrigan interrupted: "You mean to tell Harry that he should have quit when he was ahead?"

Rego: "Tell him nothing. Divert his attention to other matters. I know one thing that will work. But we must plan it well."

Harry's train came in on schedule. The absence of Rego, Fender and Harrigan didn't disturb him. Foxworth hurriedly rented a car and they both hopped in and headed for the Lodge. Harry liked Foxworth because he was so accommodating. He often felt Foxworth might be the man to succeed him if he could just teach Foxworth leadership. For one whole day on the train he lectured (as best he could) on the qualities that make for leadership.

"Leadership leads," said Harry. "For example: Don't ever say to anybody, 'What will you have'?"

"What should I say," asked Foxworth.

"Saying I'm having shrimp cocktail, New York steak, pumpkin pie and the best wine in the house!"

"Say I'm leaving work at 4:00! I'm playing golf today."

"Say: I'm in charge here. Any questions?"

Harry talked on and on. He told his theory on choosing leaders for his Divisions. Foxworth heard the legendary tale so often told by others, but never by Harry himself before. The

Leo T. McCall

story goes: A real hot, hard selling salesman in Columbus made a spectacular showing for three years running. Harry called him in to promote him. Purposely he called the salesman's wife too. Harry turned to the salesman and said:

"Ralph, I'm making you Division Manager. You'll have to move to Chicago. What do you say?"

Ralph turned to his wife and asked, "What do you think, honey?"

Honey never had the chance to accept or reject. Harry interrupted:

"Ralph! Any man who can't make up his own mind about a promotion doesn't deserve the promotion. Go back to Columbus and live as you were."

Foxworth listened attentively to all of Harry's rantings. He, like most people, could only follow, rarely lead. In the exciting years with Harry his only leading was in the anticipation of Harry's needs. This he had come to do exceedingly well. In so doing, he had, unwittingly, convinced Harry that he, Foxworth, might just be the leader to someday take over the reins of Hall & Hall and stand as firmly as Harry did not—unafraid, alone, courageously "at the bridge of the ship".

One sales manager referred not to the bridge but to the "head of the ship." He was replaced.

The lights of the marquee of the Hungry Horse Theatre blinked "Gone With the Wind". "See new wide screen version."

"Take a lesson from Rhett Butler," observed Harry. "He couldn't control Scarlet. So, he left her."

Harry knew Foxworth's wife too well and sensed that Foxworth had winced at the remark.

As they drove by the Last Chance Gulch Saloon, Harry repeated what he had so often claimed was original with him:

"One is one too many, a thousand is not enough."

Business Is Baloney

It became a chant with him as they passed bar after bar. He said it, then laughed. He slowed the car to funeral speed. Saloons stood door to door: the Lazy B, Country Club Estate, Key Club, the Buckhorn, Peace Paradise, Wild Steer, the Oxbow, Prince of Wales, Red's Rat Hole, El Cortez, Napoleon's, Run Sheep Run, Twilight Zone, Mac's, Circle K, Stagecoach Inn, Pine Cone, arrowhead, Ranger, 3 Bears, Firehole, Weary Rest, Yellowstone, Roundup, the Lariat, Twin Bears, Revelers, Travelers, Grant Vue, George's, the Flame, Silver Dollar, Log Cabin, Rainbow Inn, Cowboy, Shamrock, Silver Spur, Pink Garter, Ho-Hum, Red Arrow, Howdy Partner, Indian Village, Totem Pole, Horseshoe, Hatchet, and Dairy Queen.

Harry hated the road from the town to the Lodge. Every section climbed steeply on the outside edge of the dropoff. The Lodge sat on a plateau 9,170 feet in the sky. On the way down you could hug the mountainside while your brakes burned. Harry once let Foxworth drive up. But Foxworth believed you should step on the gas on the curve and the brake on the straight away. That may be good on the road from Little Rock to Tulsa...but not on mountainsides. So Harry drove himself, cursing all the way.

Foxworth looked around for mountain goat and bear. He was not disappointed, since he saw some of both. Harry wiped the sweat from his palms on his pants after every treacherous turn.

Foxworth handled the luggage quickly and most efficiently. Harry poured himself a rare (for him) drink. It only made him meaner. One hour later Harrigan, Fender and Rego sheepishly appeared. Harry didn't bother to say hello.

This was no rustic cabin. Pine pillars sixty feet high—20 feet apart in two columns—held a roof made of poured cement sections bolstered with rebar.

"You need plenty of oxygen up here," said Harry. On each wall was an extra supply for the giddy. But Harry believed in his heart that the big, spacious room compensated for whatever lack of oxygen there might be.

A fifteen foot wide fireplace fit the size of the room. So did a 10 foot fully-stuffed grizzly plus the largest bull moose found on the North American Continent. The pride of a Whitefish taxidermist, an Alaskan Brown Bear, stood on its hind feet in majestic silence over all.

Elk, buffalo, squirrels, mountain goats, crows, eagles, hawks, beavers, deer and chipmunks stared fixedly from their niches on the wall. For some, like the elks, buffalo and bear, only their heads showed. Others like squirrels, beavers and eagles, were intact.

No hardy AT&T man had ever strung a line across that tough mountain terrain. And of course electricity came only with thunder and lightning. Candles and lanterns played a flickering melody on the walls and over the shadows of the men. Harry cranked the old stand up victrola. It gathered momentum. Our came, "It's a Grand Old Flag."

After dinner, hastily prepared by Foxie, all sat down to five card stud.

"A dollar a chip and three raises," cautioned Harry. "And no more!" This was for Harrigan, a devout one-eyed Jacks, fives and tens wild, ace in the hole, high, low, baseball, no peek crazy man.

Harry gambled when he didn't have a dime—like the time he wrote a check for $25,000.00 to purchase raw materials—and had only $1,000.00 in the bank. He wrote the check on Friday and manipulated a loan by Monday to cover the check which promptly sailed through on Tuesday. Now a multi-millionaire, he wouldn't bet a buck unless he had aces back to back.

That night (as most times when they gambled) Harry won.

Foxworth quietly broke the victrola by winding up the spring just a little bit too tightly. Rego sat long into the night sipping a beer and nursing a pipe. Fender paced the floor for an hour and

Business Is Baloney

then fell exhausted into bed. Harrigan shook off the gambling like a veteran loser. Somehow, it would show up on his expense account.

Harry awoke when Rego went to bed.

"Search for the smokestacks! Follow the dollar! Someone is born today. Someone will die. You gotta eat. You gotta get to work. Houses need building. Operation June! Operation President's Month! Sell...sell...SELL!" With this tremendous pitch of enthusiasm Harry began the 7:00 a.m. meeting.

"Let me tell you of the time I sold cemetery lots. That was before I got smart and graduated to crypts and mausoleums. Where are you going when you're dead? To the cemetery. Right? That much we know for sure. What if you don't have a place to rest. What's your wife going to do with a dead body on her hands? She's got to get rid of it but quick. You ain't gonna leave all that responsibility to her in her hour of great need. Are you? What kind of a man are you anyway?"

"You spend good money every week for a cleaning lady to come and help your wife keep the house clean. Right" queried Harry.

"You have a garbage man take the garbage. The city sweepers clean your street. You keep your clothes clean—brush your teeth—sweep the floor and vacuum the rugs. All your life is spent keeping clean. Why are you willing to be buried in the dirt?"

From here Harry went into his pitch on the advantages of lying forever in the clean, orderly walls of a mausoleum.

Harry's point was obvious: never stop trying to better your way of life—here, now or even in the hereafter. Foxworth misinterpreted his point.

Foxworth suggested that a contest might be built around Harry's idea. Here would be something concrete in the way of inspiring the salesmen to get the job done. No one had ever made a crypt and (or) a mausoleum a prize before. It became

Leo T. McCall

difficult for anyone, including Harry himself, to object to the idea.

Fender mildly objected: "Perhaps rather than a mausoleum—money to pay for one."

Rego became analytical: "Let's examine all of the successful contests we've had in the past. Perk up Time—the prize a percolator. A trip to Las Vegas...for two. A T.V. set. A winter week in Florida...for two. A teakwood chess set. Remember, all these prized could be enjoyed by two."

"Why not two mausoleums; one for the wife and one for the husband?" interjected Foxworth.

No one could deny that Foxworth had extended Rego's logic to apply to the immediate. The whole conversation began to sound somewhat ludicrous to Harry.

"Be sure to make the mausoleum fire proof." At that sly remark of Harry's everyone started to laugh, including Harry. A cemetery lot, a crypt, a mausoleum—no one had ever made these a prize.

Rego began to hate the whole idea. Fender resolved (mentally) to quit the business and get a good job. Harrigan didn't care. He appeared quite content to be buried in dirt.

"I don't think a crypt or a mausoleum is the right prize," objected Fender.

Harry, in a rare moment of conciseness, corrected Fender:

"It's not a matter if you're right or I'm right but what is right for the company."

Turning suddenly to Harrigan, Harry asked, "What do you think Stump?"

Ever alert to avoid responsibility, Harrigan now became deliberate in all his motions. In the early days of working for the political party he had on many occasions been asked to do block work or some other unglamorous task. His repertoire of excuses

Business Is Baloney

he later put in a pamphlet, which he sold. It included such classics as:

"I have a double hernia and I couldn't carry the money."

"I lost my hearing aid and I can't hear what you are saying."

Harrigan could artfully dodge any direct question from years of actual experience. He brought the prize decision to a head simply by asking:

"Why not put it to a vote?"

And to a vote it was put. Rego, Harrigan, Foxworth and Fender all voted in favor of a crypt for making your quota and a mausoleum for exceeding it by more than 5%. After careful deliberation and considering the importance of a family prize, the prize was changed to a crypt and a mausoleum for two.

Harry voted against the whole idea, even though he had suggested it in the first place. So it was shelved.

Rego now brought forth his idea on what would keep Harry from firing Fender, at least for the time being.

"Only 6% of our sales force belongs to any lodge of any consequence. Yet those that do belong are all members of the elite of our sales force. There must be a direct relationship between success in selling glue with belonging to a Lodge. Right? Then if this is true, why not get more men into the Lodge?"

"What Lodge," asked Harry…brightening up to the idea.

"The Macknighter Lodge of course. It's the top secret and most successful lodge operating today. Everyone who is anyone belongs."

"Harry interrupted: "I don't."

In five minutes Rego had convinced Harry that he should join the Macknighter Lodge at once. To this Harry agreed. Immediately upon his return to the city he would go over and apply for membership. Rego (a 44th Macknighter) would sponsor Harry. If Harry liked the Lodge, he would agree to making memberships the prize that would lift Hall & Hall to new sales heights.

So ended the historical meeting on the mountain. All shook hands smiling.

FIVE

The Macknighter

The Macknighters held initiations on the first and third Monday nights of every month.

Two different lodges were located in the city.

Rego told Harry quite explicitly to be at the Eastern Macknighter at seven p.m., Monday night.

Harry (steeped in the Western tradition of cowboys, horses and range riding) never for a moment thought of being anything but a Western Macknighter.

Entrance to the Western Macknighter was from the rear. Harry parked his car a good block away. This was one of the rare occasions that he didn't use his chauffeur.

Before he reached the Lodge, he was accosted three different times by bums begging for money.

Peculiarly enough, all three had the same story. Each needed bus fare. And each time Harry passed out a quarter.

After the third handout, Harry made a mental note to raise hell with the city commissioners about the bus fare.

He walked into an empty corridor. No one was in sight.

Perhaps he was too early?

Maybe too late?

Rego, meanwhile, waited across town at the Eastern Macknighter hoping Harry would arrive.

Rego waited and waited and waited. Harry didn't show. Rego went home and went to bed.

Not so with Harry.

Leo T. McCall

Harry entered the Western Macknighter Lodge and should have been in the Eastern.

He entered a T-shaped corridor.

The foot of the T led to the outside where Harry entered.

The middle top of the T led to a closed door. On the left arm of the T was a clothes closet. To the right—an open door beckoned all to "enter here."

Harry hung up his camel hair overcoat and his ten gallon hat, and into the inner sanctum of Macknighter Hall he strode—unannounced, unattended and completely unnoticed.

In the history of the Macknighter secret Lodge no one had ever entered the inner sanctum who was not a qualified member. Someone had goofed.

In the dimly lit room Harry blinked. He wandered around the ceremonial table taking a curious look at a skeleton head, a gun and a pumpkin.

It reminded him of Halloween.

Strangers looked befuddled. Others recognized Harry. Maybe from a picture in the paper, or a Junior Chamber of Commerce bulletin, or a personal interview.

Harry grinned at those who knew him and they in turn grinned back.

"This is the initiation?" Harry asked himself.

In the eerie atmosphere, in the shroud of secrecy, with such aloof treatment Harry began to sense the beginning of the initiation ceremony.

Did you initiate yourself? Harry began to think so.

Ridiculous!

After a half hour he began to drift unheeded among the initiators.

Harry had little conscience on major matters and none of the matters inconsequential.

Business Is Baloney

But the more he wandered the more he felt that this was something big.

But it was not going right.

Harry went back to the door through which he had entered.

By now a guard stood alert and ready to accept only those who knew the password of the evening.

The guard was one of Harry's office help. He could not believe that Harry was not a member of the Macknighters.

"Jerry," said Harry recognizing the man. "How do I get initiated into this Lodge?"

"Boss, you must be kidding."

"I'm not kidding," growled Harry. "Where's Rego?"

"Haven't seen him, Boss. Not tonight, anyway."

The guard, Jerry Footmaker, had never seen the Boss at a Western Macknighter meeting before, but he assumed Harry must be a member.

It was even more difficult for Jerry to believe because Harry was already in the ceremonial room. Footmaker laughed disbelievingly when Harry repeated the question:

"Where in the hell is the initiation?"

Footmaker drew back his head to check out Harry on his bifocals. Sure enough, it was Harry all right.

"The initiation room, Boss?"

"That's right. The initiation room. I'm joining up."

Jerry grinned and laughed again.

"Don't kid me, Boss. I know you are a member already. I saw you at the St. Patrick's dance. Quit the clowning."

"You never saw me at any dance...St. Patrick's or St. Vitus. How, where do I go?"

With this Harry brushed by Footmaker and stepped back into the T-shaped hall. Harry had allegiance to no one.

He made his own rules.

Leo T. McCall

He never liked the idea of secrecy, the Lodge, or the waste of time.

He had done this just for Rego.

And Rego wasn't even there.

Come to think of it, where was Rego?

He blinked his eyes again as he bolted back into the well-lit hall.

"That silent treatment for the last half hour in there wasn't part of the initiation, was it?"

"What silent treatment?"

"Back there around the skull." This time Harry spoke brusquely. Jerry's face again showed bewilderment. But, he reasoned, surely Harry couldn't be serious. Harry was not known to be a funny man nor one to make practical jokes.

"I know you're kidding."

Now Jerry made up his mind that Harry couldn't be an executive of a large company like Hall & Hall and not be a Macknighter. Everybody who was anybody was a Macknighter.

Just then two men entered and passed by Jerry, but not before whispering something in his ear. Harry was so close he couldn't help but hear the password: "Whiffenpoof."

Then a Macknighter in a silver flowing, floor-length gown stuck his head out into the hallway. Across his chest a dragon spouted fire. In his right hand he carried a silver sword. In the left hand he held a 38 caliber revolver. This obvious anarchism puzzled Harry.

"Everybody here a Macknighter?" he asked. Everybody could only include Jerry and Harry—the only ones standing in the hall. The question was a natural one, since the man had never seen Harry before.

"He's O.K.," said Jerry nodding his head at Harry.

"He's from the Eastern Macknighter Lodge."

Business Is Baloney

"Good. Maybe he can help out tonight. We're short one initiator."

Harry, now completely befuddled, realized that Jerry honestly believed him to be a member of the highly secretive, worldwide, Macknighter Lodge, and he could do nothing to dissuade him.

He tried again.

"I'm sure he'll agree to help. Won't you boss?"

"I'm telling you for the last time, Footmaker, I came to be initiated myself. Now, what do I do and where do I go?"

At this outburst the head Macknighter looked apprehensively at Jerry.

"Ha...Ha...Ha...quite a kidder. You can rely on him, oh mighty high potentate."

With this assurance the mighty high potentate ducked back into the ceremonial room.

"Stand guard will you, boss?" asked Jerry of Harry. "I'll go fetch you a robe."

With this, Jerry promptly disappeared in the semi-darkness of the inner sanctum and Harry was left standing alone to guard a highly secretive meeting, and Initiation night also!

It was most peculiar that he couldn't get through to Footmaker that he was *not* a member of any Macknighter Loge—that he was Harry Hall, President of the largest glue factory in the world and nothing more.

Now, here he was guarding the entrance to a most secretive meeting.

It disturbed Harry to think an employee of his was obviously a dunderhead. He made a mental note to find out who had hired him and what had happened to Hall & Hall's highly respected prescreening applicant tests.

Leo T. McCall

Two men entered. Both hung their coats and hats on the rack. First one, then the other whispered to Harry, "Whiffenpoof."

Each then slipped silently through the doorway and into the inner sanctum—the Ceremonial Initiation Room. Harry, now deep in thought, never gave either one a second thought.

A moment later another man entered the main doorway. He carried a suitcase. This he put down in the closet. He carefully hung his coat and hat on the hat rack. He crossed over the hallway and approached Harry.

"Good evening, sir. I'm Jim Hawkins from the International Club in Peoria." After this he dug into his billfold.

"Good evening. How are you?" was Harry's brief return.

"Here are my Peoria Cub credentials." At this Hawkins handed Harry his International Macknighter card.

"What do you want me to do about it," asked Harry.

"Well, sir, I'm just in town overnight. I didn't have anything to do so I thought I could spend the evening at the club."

"Go ahead," gruffly replied Harry. "It's your club. Not mine."

At this the stranger placed his identification card back in his billfold.

"But don't I need a password? I've already given you my card. I gave you the sign. Now will you give me the password?"

"What sign are you talking about?" rasped Harry.

"The sign. The sign." With this Hawkins of Peoria went through all the mysterious signals that anybody in the Macknighters would recognize instantly.

Harry pushed him impatiently into the Inner Sanctum. Just as he did, someone opened the door that until now had been closed all evening—the door where the "to be initiated" sat in sullen silence. A smiling, jolly old fellow of about 50 came to Harry.

Business Is Baloney

"Say, sir, we are missing one more recruit. Maybe you can help me."

"Try me." Harry now had lost his patience completely.

"Well, this man's name is Harry Hall. No one can find him here." He pointed over his shoulder toward the room that divided that hat closet from the Inner Sanctum.

"Never heard of him."

"Well, we'll just have to go ahead without him."

With this the jolly old fellow stepped back into the room.

Jerry Footmaker appeared from the Ceremonial Room with a long robe. Harry had now given up any hope of using this Lodge as prize for his salesmen. Unimpressed by the bungling procedure, exasperated beyond words, he silently let Jerry help him into the robe. Mentally he decided to leave as soon as he could but allowed Jerry to point him toward the Inner Sanctum with the remark: "Have Fun."

Harry didn't know whether to laugh, play along or expose the whole mistaken affair. Actually he felt hurt. If a few had recognized the President of Hall & Hall they were unimpressed. He decided to play along as long as he could without revealing the obvious fact, to him at least, that he was initiating new members of the Macknighter Lodge without being a member himself.

He gracefully accepted Jerry's assistance as he donned the cape but he burned within. Harry went through the motions of the man in front of him—up to a point.

Harry was unimpressed by the whole affair until someone (he never did know who) pulled a gun. Harry promptly floored the guy with an uppercut. Bedlam ensued. Someone (later thought to be a recruit) called the police.

Harry escaped before the police came. A small article in the next morning's newspaper reported the incident as just another police run. Three thousand dollars in damage was done to the

Leo T. McCall

interior of the Macknighter Lodge. Walls were broken down, not to speak of doors, windows and sacred symbols.

Rego, sleeping peacefully through the night, didn't know what happened until he read the paper the next morning. As usual he read the whole newspaper as he did each morning, reporting to Harry any newsworthy event.

This incident he never brought up nor did he ever mention it to Harry again.

SIX

Down on the Farm

Harry continued to go through the motions. Everything he did for the next two months he had done before. No reason why it wouldn't work again. But it didn't.

Sales plunged downward and downward again. By mid-May, the pattern was set. Hall and Hall, fast losing its hold on the glue market, became destined to be second-rate.

A stockholders meeting offered shareholders no great promise for the future. Each recognized the set pattern of the meeting which was always rehearsed days before, which always ended on a high optimistic note for the future. Harry again would be at the head of the ship. All ill-timed news release reported the minutes of the meeting in the morning papers on the day of the meeting. By late afternoon, the public relations department of Hall and Hall was boarded up and closed forever. Harry denied that it ever existed.

"We must go down on the farm," declared Harry firmly on May 25th. Later, appropriately on Memorial Day, he made it official in the company news vehicle— "Business Builder."

This meant he was taking direct action, personally, for the farm was his, not the company's. It meant he would personally foot the bills. It was his last, most generous contribution to the business. It didn't seem fair that the barn should burn down at the height of the meeting and the horses be allowed to run away.

The theme of Harry's Down on the Farm show, "The Circus Comes to Town," intrigued all who were fortunate enough to be invited.

Leo T. McCall

Orian Wakefield directed, as he had the Silver Jubilee. Russ Fender controlled the center ring.

Harry often said that selling was 99% enthusiasm and 1% know-how. He felt that one magnificent move on his part could spur his managers to even greater heights than they ever had attained before and now was the time to do it. So he called all 60 managers in from all parts of the country plus all seven Divisional Vice Presidents, all of the bankers who at one time or another had loaned him money to carry on the business, all local newspaper people, all inside brass of Hall and Hall and radio and top T.V. personalities in the local community.

"My kind of enthusiasm knows no bounds. Give me a thousand just like me and I'll give you the greatest business in the world," Harry had often said.

Many felt Harry overlooked many salient feature of selling in stressing enthusiasm. A few more thoughtful employees from time to time pointed out that competition was getting rougher as the years went by. Price was beginning to play quite a factor in loss of sales, and know-how on the part of competition seemed to be on the increase. While other glue concerns seemed to stress product knowledge, planned selling, complete coverage and trained salesmen, Harry continued to preach his gospel of unbounded enthusiasm. And his close, highly paid disciples like Rego, Foxworth, Ribbon and James, like well trained dog teams, continued to follow their lead dog.

Harry called in the local zookeeper to determine what he could offer them from his animal kingdom. The keeper couldn't turn him down since Harry practically supported the Zoo alone.

It came to three elephants, one giraffe, five seals, two lions, two tigers, one panther, four bears, three cubs, and four peacocks. Harry would use his high school company band. He could get clowns from his administrative department. Trapeze artists must be hired along with a few tightrope walkers. Harry honestly felt that with the excitement created by a steam calliope playing spirited music, real animals on parade, men on the flying

Business Is Baloney

trapeze, and wild animals roaring in their cages, that Hall and Hall again could lead all competition in the now very sticky glue business.

A big tent was not necessary. Harry's big horse barn would be adequate. The quarter horse could be stabled with the cows until after the show.

In the frenzied weeks that followed, few of the inside personnel stuck to the glue business. All became involved in readying Harry's barn for the circus.

Fender spent three weeks preparing for his role as ringmaster. Les James spent three weeks in the library studying as much as he could fine on Emmett Kelly, Felix Adler and Paul Sung. James, naturally, would lead the clowns.

Harry had talked Harrigan into taming the local lions and cats during the show. Harrigan took a dim view of this but seemed assured that all would go well when the zookeeper promised to keep the animals well-fed.

John Rego would be "Buffalo Bill Cody" and Harry's wife, Nellie, would be Annie Oakley.

Foxworth volunteered to swing once from the trapeze. Harry gave him two weeks off to travel with the Wallenda family.

Tom Ribbon would have one assignment, fire chief. A little house would be set fire as a climax to the show and Ribbon would enter in a red fire wagon and promptly put the fire out.

Harry himself would play P.T. Barnum.

The house burning didn't appeal to Harry. The closest fire barn was twenty miles away. But Fender assured him that it was a small house—that Ribbon could practically spit on it and extinguish it. Probably someone should have thought of what a quarter horse will do in the case of fire.

Posters prepared by Harry's ad agency billed the meeting as the "Greatest Show on Earth." Advance notices to that effect

Leo T. McCall

were in the hands of every District Manager two weeks in advance of the meeting date.

The cast for the show, including participants and workers, musicians, and office help numbered 100. Harry's barn was made into a huge circus ring and every seat was ringside.

On arrival, each District Manager was escorted to the impromptu bar set up back of the "Big Top" barn. Stimulating calliope music blared from atop a music wagon. In an hour's cocktail time almost any Manager would have gone into the lion's cage with Harrigan had he chickened out. But Harrigan already was one hour ahead of them with the drinking—and, feeling little pain, needed no prodding to enter the cage. Fender started the show with the typical ringmaster's whistle followed by a short blast of the band. Normally a circus starts with a parade, but it was thought best to get the lion act over with and the lion out of the way.

Harrigan was led to the door of the cage by the zookeeper.

The zookeeper let in his two lions, his two tigers and his one panther. Each animal leaped into position atop its assigned stool. The panther, logged down with his sixth meal of the day, had trouble reaching his position atop the four foot stool. On the third try he made it.

Harrigan stared fixedly, first at the lions, then the tigers and lastly the panther. H e raised his whip back over his head. The sudden motion threw him flat on his back. A shriek went up from a sober few. The animals appeared to be disinterested.

Harrigan arose, wiped the sawdust off his blue silk shirt and tan breaches. The older lion of the two looked the least ferocious as Harrigan approached him. He drew his pistol and fired it. The lion, deafened many years ago by pistol shots, never blinked an eye.

Harrigan then defiantly weaved a path in and out between them all. The unsteadiness of his footwork baffled them. The two cats took a playful swipe at him.

Business Is Baloney

Harrigan again flipped his whip back over his shoulder, this time catching it on one of the bars. He spun around. In jerky motion he tried to pull the whip loose but instead pulled the cage down on top of him and the lions and cats.

The animals looked for a way out. The zookeeper lifted the bars, freeing the animals long enough to allow them to crawl out of the center ring and back into their private cars. Harrigan had to be carried out.

The seals did all right, but Foxworth was something else again. He had spent two wonderful weeks traveling with the flying Wallendas. Their friendliness, high spirits, and amazing courage inspired him. He worked very hard during those two weeks. Each morning he worked with the barbells. Each afternoon he took long jaunts to strengthen his leg muscles. Each night, after watching the magnificent family perform, he did push-ups to strengthen his arms. Never in his life had he felt so good, so trim, so physically fit.

He had to do one thing. He had to swing from a twenty foot pedestal and in mid-air catch the arms of a local strong man coming to him on another swing. After watching the routine manner of the flying Wallendas do the same thing as just a warm up, he felt he'd have no trouble duplicating this fundamental swing of any flying trapeze artist. He felt that practice wasn't necessary.

Very hurriedly the cats and lions were driven off. The cage was disassembled and the twenty foot high wire was put up.

In gratitude to his boss for the trip, Foxworth insisted no net would be needed. So no net was installed.

A local strong boy climbed to his pedestal, hung from his knee and swung out over the center ring for a few warm ups.

Fender entered the ring, blew his whistle and signaled for a fan-fare. After the music, the lights were blacked out for five seconds. When they came back on, Foxworth stood in the center ring dressed in a flaming red cape with a brilliant smile. Fender

Leo T. McCall

gave him a typical "daring young man" introduction. On Fender's signal, Foxworth flung off the cape, revealing a trim figure in red tights and white tennis shoes. He quickly ascended the twenty-foot rope to his pedestal opposite the local strong boy. He flashed a courageous smile and looked down at his appreciative audience. And right there he froze to the rope. The local strong boy swung over the tried to extricate him but didn't have enough strength to pry Foxworth's hands loose. Fender climbed up and attempted to help. The two together couldn't get him off the rope.

After ten minutes of wrestling with Foxie, Fender slid down and talked momentarily to Harry. Both beckoned to Rego to come over and enter into the discussion. Rego left the arena. Fender left but came back in one minute with three horse blankets. He signaled for help.

"We'll have to shoot him down," he told the audience. "We can't go on with the show with him hanging up there."

He spread out the three blankets and stacked them over each other.

"Give me a hand," he said. "I'll need about ten men. We'll catch him fireman-fashion in the blankets."

Rego returned armed with a 30-30 Winchester. As the men held the blankets directly below Fender, Rego began firing away at the ropes just above Foxie. Foxie just continued to grin. On the eleventh shot Rego blasted the rope in two and Foxie fell safely into the blanket.

Les James was on next with all his clowns from the Administrative department; the comptroller, the credit manager, the auditors and the chief accountant plus the office manager. James wore three inflated inner tubes around his stomach under his clown uniform. All his understudies pricked him with long needles which deflated the rubber tubes to the delight of all, especially the understudies who had been wanting to prick their waxen man for many years.

Business Is Baloney

James then gave a serious talk on the inflated dollar, the importance of being able to borrow money, the need for better budget control and how "we must all tighten our belts for the obvious rough times that lie ahead." All in all it depressed everyone.

The giraffe led by the V.P. in charge of promotion carried a placard hanging from his ear that read: "Let's stick our necks out too. We need the sales."

A peacock followed the giraffe with a placard: "Strut your stuff." Another followed with the sign: "Be proud of our glue, it's the best in the world." A third peacock carried the motto: "I'm all puffed up over the new glue line" and the last peacock carried a sign that had hastily been thrown on upside down and no one ever did figure out what it said. But the peacock surely was beautiful.

Departmental heads from all the subdivisions and subsidiaries of Hall and Hall gave skits for an hour tying their assignments in with the "Greatest Show on Earth."

The last act of the day, before Ribbon was to set fire to the little red house, was to be Harry's wife leading fourteen of Harry's quarter horses around the center ring in a gallop. Timing was such that it would be necessary to put the little red house in the center ring before the quarter horses entered. Then the quarter horses would swing around it as the band played and as Nellie rode bareback atop the charger "Hurrying Hall" and Nellie in her Annie Oakley costume would shoot blanks from a 30-30 Winchester at a target in the ceiling. The target was four ducks and after each shot a duck would fall.

The little red house actually was full of hay sprayed with gasoline. Ribbon was merely to start the red house on fire by shooting a blank cartridge at close range. He didn't have to.

Nellie came blasting in on cue followed by Harry's 14 quarter horses. She made one complete circle before all 14 were in line. Just as she prepared to take her first shot, she slipped,

Leo T. McCall

the gun went off, but not upward. It blasted right into the red house setting it on fire.

The horses bolted in unison for the big barn door.

Everyone fled. No one thought about the red fire engine. And as the barn burned down and as Nellie disappeared over the farthermost hill followed by Harry's 14 quarter horses, Rego, the deepest thinker with the most penetrating mind of anyone at Hall and Hall, was heard to say, "I'd like to see Ringling Bros. Barnum & Bailey top this."

SEVEN

Choose, Hamilton and Loose

In the twilight of a brilliant career, Harry's star began to descend. Other stars trailing in Harry's orbit began to descend too.

Les James stepped forward to make an honest suggestion.

"Harry, and I say this sincerely, is it not time to evaluate the budget? Isn't it obvious that Fender can do nothing to stop our plunging sales?"

Harry just burned.

"Remember, Harry, we had a going deal at thirty million. A hundred is out of sight. Why don't we just budget for a comfortable thirty million?"

Harry burned some more.

Harry yelled for Rego.

Rego suggested that it was time to bring the business consultant into the company to examine Les James' administrative division. Perhaps a cut in the budget would come from there.

James' negative thinking had to be curtailed at once.

The next day, in came Choose, Hamilton and Loose.

And the fun began.

They questioned everybody from the janitor to Harry.

Their final recommendation. Fire Harry!

It had taken them two months and thirty thousand dollars to come to this conclusion.

Leo T. McCall

EIGHT

Reunion at the Como Zoo

Who thought of the reunion at the Como Park Zoo nobody could determine. But of all the invitations sent out, only a few refused. And those few had been long gone to other parts of the country or were dead.

The idea appealed to Harry. Harry had many memories of the Zoo and of the adjacent Como Lake area.

The reunion would be in the summertime when the monkeys were out on the island. It would include all his grade school classmates—the girls and the boys.

It would be as harmless as a Nancy Drew mystery.

Harry had been a chief proponent of the Zoo. He had been the Zoo's best contributor. And Harry would receive accolades.

So he thought.

He was most anxious to see the best-looking girl in the eighth grade again—Eleanor Farrell.

Occasionally he wondered what had happened to the Eleanor of his youth. Had she married?

Was she still a beauty? Or had age eroded those sparkling eyes, that curly black hair, the dimpled chin and girlish figure?

Time alone would tell the only story to tell.

The old Como Gang would be together again.

Oh, how Harry had labored over contributions to the Zoo.

Harry didn't want to hear the success stories. He was the top success.

Business Is Baloney

From the last dog on the sled team he had become the lead dog...the only dog who knew where he was headed.

His public relations department ordered monogrammed playing cards for all who said they were coming.

Little did it matter that some didn't play cards.

The Como Zoo meant fond memories for Harry. Here at the Zoo he had had one of his first chances to count "out of state" license plates and dream of far off places like Michigan and Utah and Canada.

And here at the Zoo he saw many animals that were look-a-likes to his old school chums.

Harry, as he became more affluent in the community, contributed much to the success of the Zoo. There was much to tell all his old school mates.

He could tell them of how he instigated the control fence around the Zoo...not to keep the animals in but the gatecrashers out.

Harry could tell how he brought Spanky, the trained seal, to the Zoo. He could also tell about how he obtained a pair of Platypuses of some questionable value, who, as they attained adulthood, increased in value. However, much to Harry's concern, the pair disappeared one night in the Como Lake mud.

Harry reminisced as he thought of the Reunion. He would tell of his gallant fight to bring a bigger and better Zoo to old St. Paul.

He reread his historic statement to the Zoological Society:

"The aim of Harry Hall is to bring Como Park into the next decade with a modern and substantial Zoological Garden on the order of similar institutions in San Diego, Portland and Salt Lake City. I will make available the following to the Twin City public:

A. Educational, cultural and research opportunities for young and old alike, to study representative animal, bird and aquatic life for maximum benefits.
B. Recreational facilities and services inherent to the modern concept of a zoological park.
C. Additional and easily accessible parking lots.
D. Expanded family services such as picnic grounds, guides, nurses, wading pools, shelters, Kiddie Zoo and related activities.
E. A prestige attraction which will provide absorbing interest not only for the citizens of St. Paul but also for visitors from throughout the world.

Harry would point out how he took a dilapidated mess from a worn out Volunteer Committee at the Zoo and brought the Zoo to new heights.

And what a mess it had been. When appointed to guide the Zoo's return to respectability Harry took a trip through old Como Zoo. He saw animals and birds not in their natural habitat, but behind bars and in cages just as they had been presented in ancient Rome.

He saw no natural surroundings except the waterfowl pool fronting the main cage building. A $10,000 gorilla, a magnificent specimen, rolled on a floor in a welter of used popcorn boxes licking off the salt. He saw the finest Siberian tigers in captivity presented in box-like cages barely large enough for them to turn around and exercise. He blinked at a pair of beautiful snow leopards hardly seen against a background of the same color. Nowhere was there an adequate explanation of the various animals species and their place in the world. A few beat-up looking eagles and hawks had lost their feathers in drab cages that were a disgrace. Concessions were packed so closely that the blaring of music and noise of drums and roller coasters

Business Is Baloney

distracted the tranquility. The concessions had to be set apart from the Zoo proper, this much Harry knew.

Gibbon monkeys, a fine exhibit of acrobatic animals, found it difficult to keep healthy in crowded surroundings. A snake or two was the reptile exhibit. In truth, when Harry took over, Como Zoo was "over the hill".

Minnesota, a great fishing state, had not one aquarium. Minnesota had no exhibit of its wild life. The citizens had been too occupied with schools, water, sewer, libraries, and other public services to think about creating a major zoological park.

When Harry became chairman, the animal fund was a mere $6,000. You couldn't buy more than a llama, a kangaroo, a rhesus monkey, a mandrill, a whitetail deer or red fox for that small amount.

When Harry had finished his drive for a bigger and better Zoo, the animal kingdom abounded with gorillas, chimps, spotted leopards, pelicans, Egyptian geese, white crested laughing thrushes, gold fronted Chloropses, Kodiak bears, Indian elephants, striped hyenas (sex undetermined), Sicilian donkeys, deodorized skunks, mouflon sheep, Texas longhorns, adult baboons, sidewinders, boa constrictors, chestnut-breasted teals, Canadian wolves, kangaroos, alligators, jungle-bred Royal Bengal tigers, and a king vulture or two.

Harry employed many of his fine assistants in his building program for the Zoo. Some alert assistants even found the cooperation of a Women's Auxiliary to do things that the men would not attempt. In this way, Harry felt he was liberating women.

The women talked one large church into promoting a rummage sale. The women raised $2,800.00, clear profit. Boy Scouts started a tag day—the tag being in the form of a small tiger which hundreds of Boy Scouts sold on the streets of St. Paul for two weekends in a row.

Leo T. McCall

Harry heard that a Swedenborgian church had a huge treasury just sitting dormant. He talked the head Pastor into persuading the Board of Directors of the Church to contribute money to the Zoo. Immediately other church denominations felt left out and insisted on making donations to the Zoo.

Harry named (and rightly so) one of the camels in the Zoo Minnie, for Minneapolis. He had hoped to get the Sister City citizens interested. But Minnie died.

The ploy worked, but not in a way that Harry had expected.

Immediately on the death of Minnie, the Mayor of Minneapolis issued the following proclamation:

"WHEREAS, the citizens of the City of Minneapolis have learned of the untimely passing of 'Minnie', the Como Zoo camel named for Minneapolis; and

WHEREAS, her mate, 'Paul', named after our Sister City, Saint Paul, has become a forlorn and lonely spouse; and

WHEREAS, the cities of Saint Paul and Minneapolis recognize that their interests are common and that they are one metropolitan unit; and

WHEREAS, the citizens of Minneapolis wish to perpetuate this inter-city understanding and helpfulness,

NOW, THEREFORE, I, K.P. Pioski, Mayor of the City of Minneapolis, do hereby urge all of the people of our city to help purchase a mate for "Paul" by contributing what they can to the Como Zoo Volunteer Committee, in the care of Minneapolis Chamber of Commerce, Minneapolis 2, Minnesota."

Respectfully yours,
K.P. Pieski, Mayor

Business Is Baloney

With his seal of approval, the Honorable Mayor of Minneapolis, captured donations from all who had ever loved and lost.

Harry had much with which to impress his former classmates. He had done so much for the good of the Como Zoo. He personally contributed a souvenir guidebook to the Zoo. He posed for pictures promoting the Zoo: Harry in front of the lion cage; Harry standing by a caged porcupine; Harry with a raven on his shoulder; Harry tossing a rubber ball to the trained seal; Harry playing catch with a chimpanzee; Harry feeding the swans; Harry hugging a doe; Harry bottle-feeding a lion cub; and his last public picture—Harry gingerly petting a cheetah's tail.

But none of these contributions compared to the work he had done in getting the "big shots" of his city to help support the Zoo drive for money.

Archie Brush came through not only with money but a trained chimp act, an emu, of crossword puzzle fame, a sulphur-breasted toucan with a banana beak, a jabiru stork and his own pet panda.

Stan Hobard came out one day to the Zoo and milked a goat, sheared a sheep and caught fish in the moat surrounding Monkey Island.

Don Doutan, from Minneapolis, got the Director of the National Zoological Society to come to his "Twin Cities Zoo."

But when Harry heard Doutan mention a greater Twin City Zoo, he got Doutan removed from the committee. "Como Zoo is in St. Paul—not the Twin Cities" stormed Harry.

"Minneapolis," raged Harry, "is making another attempt to get something for nothing. They are trying to get a zoo which they now don't have and charge half the costs to St. Paul, if not all the costs!"

During his active campaign for the Zoo, Harry came to be known as "Dr. Harry" because he loved children and animals.

Leo T. McCall

A friendly widow of Harry's acquaintance, Mrs. W. Q. Lillian thought so much of Harry's plans for a greater Zoo that she gave the Zoo a fitting memorial to her late husband—a baby elephant.

A retired Minnesotan (living in Florida) who had made his fortune with a local sandpaper company gave the Zoo what he considered an appropriate animal for Minnesota's climate—an Antarctic penguin.

Harry surely had a lot to tell his old schoolmates about what he did for the Zoo. Just before the Reunion he started to reminisce about "the good old days."

What would the "old classmates" look like now? How many had kept out of jail from the old gang? Harry's heart was still with the Zoo. Maybe a few of his classmates could throw in a few bucks and for a $1,000 become a Patron or, like Harry, throw in $10,000 and become a Benefactor!

But on his mind more than the boys was Eleanor Farrell. Had she married? Was she a nun? What had happened to her since that time (the last time Harry had talked to her) when she had called him to go bike riding around Como Park Lake?

Harry liked the way she tap-danced. She even toe-danced! And she surely had a sweet smile.

The other girls from the class faded as in a mist from his memory. Most were taller than the boys. When they lined up for the class photo, the boys stood in the first three rows...their arms held rigidly to their black-belted white pants with white shirts with two red roses pinned to the shirt pocket over their hearts.

The girls stood on the school steps in the background. Of course, they were not allowed to smile. Only Eleanor got away with a semblance of a smile and one boy whom they couldn't control smiled openly—that was George O'Phelan—voted later in his college career as the most likely to succeed.

Business Is Baloney

Everyone was to meet at the railing surrounding the moat to Monkey Island. From there Harry would take his "old classmates" on a tour of the Zoo. After that all would go inside the Como Park Conservatory for pictures.

Then a rented city bus would take all down to Mitch's for lunch—lunch being on Mitch.

This at least was the plan.

Over the years there had been much bickering between Minneapolis and St. Paul, which Harry thought was foolish. Certainly there was not room for two Zoos in the Twin Cities. Children, at the age when they are interested in animals, would not be bothered by where the Zoo was located. Harry thought it best for the rest of the Twin Cities to take the same view, especially with the Zoo being in St. Paul.

Harry's P.R. man had filled Harry with jingles that even Hollywood and Disney would envy.

"Never smile at a crocodile" and "do you wanna buy a boa" were two of the expressions.

The first to arrive at the Reunion was Tommy Fitzgerald, the smallest kid in the class, but the one with the biggest ideas. Before Harry could grasp his hand, he told Harry what to do with the Zoo.

"Go underground with it!" exclaimed old Fitz.

Old Fitz now looked like a Leprechaun.

"Nothing like an underground zoo has ever been tried. You will experience the feeling of entering a cave and you will follow a winding underground course. Nocturnal animals should be exhibited in their natural habitat.

"Beavers can be observed building a dam plus swimming under water. You must have a bat cave, a blindfish cave and a mushroom cave. Put in special lighting that won't annoy the animals. Other animals that go underground can be exhibited, like prairie dogs, bear, aardvark and kinkajou."

Leo T. McCall

Harry thought to himself that probably the reason old Fitz never got married was of his obsession with underground animals.

Old Fitz never gave a dime to help the Zoo committee buy any animals but he did give a lot of advice.

Eleanor Farrell had married Shorty Dillion. This Harry did not know.

But Harry did know Shorty Dillion. Shorty was the fastest ice-skater on Como Lake. And the best hockey player of all the Como Gang. He even had a tryout in Montreal—an awesome feat for an American in those old days when all the major league hockey player were Canadians.

But Shorty's penchant for barroom brawls had kept him in the minor leagues. And in his more mature age he became an excellent bargaining agent for the Teamsters, thanks a great deal to his hockey training on Como Lake.

For the Reunion, Shorty came with his lovely wife, Eleanor, even though he was younger than Eleanor and shouldn't have come to Harry's class reunion. He had never been in Harry's class.

So many years had passed by that Harry did not recognize Eleanor when she arrived…with Shorty.

At the time Eleanor arrived, Harry was standing by the moat, his ten gallon hat jauntily pushed back from his forehead and his right elbow curled around the railing that circled Monkey Island.

Harry was talking to Marie Borschen. Marie was showing Harry the class picture. They were engaged in a game of identification. In her mind she held a teacher's pointer.

Little, slim Marie was still little, slim Marie and because she had retained her girlish figure, she was the only one with nerve enough to bring the old picture of the class. Oh how beautiful they looked—then.

"Harry," said Marie. "You know who I am in the picture because I haven't changed at all." Then she pointed to herself on

Business Is Baloney

the photo. And Harry did have to admit she hadn't changed much.

"Marie," observed Harry. "Your hair does have a glint of red in it, now. But how fortunate for you. You are not gray or bald. What is your secret of eternal youth?"

To Harry's surprise she answered honestly.

"I do all my own housework."

Because of some biological quirk, the boys (at graduation time) had outnumbered the girls two to one. But, when the final count would be made of the Reunion years later, the girls would outnumber the boys.

As chairman, Marie had made contact with every member of the class. It was depressing to Harry to hear her tell him how so many of the boys he knew were now dead.

Unnoticed by Harry and Marie was a fat figure of notoriety—who came quietly into the Reunion. And not even classmates could guess the once "most likely to succeed" boy who had grown fat and gray and slow moving.

Joe Schurr had become a priest and then a bishop and from there, as far as the public was concerned, he had gone downhill. He married a divorcee.

But he still had the charming smile, although the wit had gone. He associated himself with the more sober things in life—like Ms. This and Ms. That. And how nice it was that Ms. This and Ms. That knew where she stood in the order of the Universe. How nice it was that Ms. Found herself and Joe got lost.

And then the "least likely to succeed" came. Gerald Grazinski could only be remembered by his classmates for dirty shirts, scuffed shoes, a quizzical look and bowl haircut. At that time nobody had discovered deodorant, least of all Grazinski.

But Grazinski had married well. Not wealth, but a German housekeeper who kept him well groomed, tidy and on time. And that is the way he now ran his airline.

Leo T. McCall

When Harry spotted Grazinski, he was talking to Shorty Dillion and a little gray-haired old lady. Also with Grazinski, Dillion and the gray-haired old lady was Rick Hokmanson. Rick was in charge, as he had been back in the good old school days when he was voted the best prospective politician. And politician he had become. Rick had grown a beard, knowing the public assumed that anyone with a beard had a brain. He also had taken on a slight foreign accent which Americans also associated with brains. So they and the rest of the fair city kept voting good old Rich into office—any office he chose—the current one being representative to the state legislature. But Rich had become vindictive. And his charming smile had become a snarl.

Harry never cared for him and didn't talk to him.

Grazinski had taken the little gray haired girl by the arm and led over to Harry.

"Remember Eleanor Farrell?" Grazinski asked Harry.

"Yes, what about her?"

"Harry," smile Grazinski. "This is Eleanor Farrell."

Harry looked at the little old lady in disbelief. He remembered Eleanor Farrell as he last saw her when she was fourteen. This gray haired, plump, smiling old lady just couldn't be the same.

"You're not Eleanor Farrell?" in amazement.

"You're not Eleanor Farrell?" This time Harry started to laugh.

Shorty Dillion took offense at Harry's smiling attitude. And when Harry for the last time said, "You're not Eleanor Farrell," laughing until he cried with tears, Shorty hit him with a Sunday punch in the back of the neck, picked him up bodily and threw Harry into the moat.

This ended the Reunion.

NINE

Goal Line Stand

Slowly and surely the old familiar faces that Rego had known so long slipped upstairs and shut the door.

And the tick, tick, tock of the stately clock in Rego's hall tolled Rego's eminent departure. Although we know not what hour it will come, it will surely come and Harry knew too well that his days were numbered too.

And like all of us not ready to go, Rego drifted back in his mind's eye to the days of his youth and the glory that never was but could have been.

Many an hour he had chartered the glorious days of the Gopher's Golden era in football. Radio broadcasters screamed the excitement of goal line stands and last second tough down runs. And the statistics of each game became common talk and extremely vital to all who pretended to know what football was all about.

Before each Gopher game, Rego would rule out (on the back of whatever paper was around) the dimensions of a football field. The width just half the length and a line for the five, ten and so on to the fifty yard line and then back down the other side from the fifty to the forty five and right to the goal line. All of this taken care of, he would sit in front of the magic voice box and wait the start of the game.

The most pleasant sound in Rego's world came from a table model Crosley radio. Each Saturday afternoon he held his ear to the "voice box" awaiting the referee's whistle starting the Gopher game of the week.

Leo T. McCall

The frantic voice of the announcer screaming through the background of Minnesota Hats Off to Thee" was more real than ever seeing it in person.

Every punt return, every yard gained, every penalty, and every pass had a symbol on the chart and the complete game itself could be read from the records kept by the young football-hungry fans.

A new hero came by every year. And the heroes of old were soon forgotten, replaced by soon to be forgotten new ones. That's football.

And oh! how statistics meant so much. Who had the most first downs? Who had the best punt returns? Who was penalized most? Who had the longest gain from rushing? Who had the most and longest gains from passing? Who fumbled? Who didn't? What was the average kickoff return? Who recovered the fumbles? What was Minnesota's longest gain from running or passing? What was the average punt return?

Who won?

Johnny Rego had grown up with Harry in the old Como Gang.

Rego had gone on to college and had become a football hero for one magic moment in three years of holding down the bench.

But when all "his strength failed him at length" and he lay on his death bed, he called for Harry. And Harry came.

A stroke had taken Rego's vision. But he could still hear. Rego had refused to go to a hospital and in his stubbornness had insisted that all the lights in his room be turned on even though it was 1 o'clock in the afternoon according to his radio.

"Read to me, Harry," Rego whispered.

"Read what?"

Rego pulled open the drawer in the table next to his bed. From it he took out a yellow, tattered newspaper.

"This."

Business Is Baloney

And ever so gently Rego handed Harry the last words he wanted to hear in this "vale of tears".

With the lights on and the sun from the windows blinding him, Harry squinted to read. The old yellow newspaper started to fall apart in his hands.

But as it did Harry read:

> "Irish Squeeze Pas the Army,
> Purdue Hands Iowa 3rd Defeat,
> Badgers Down Illini,
> State Drops Wildmen 13-12 on Rego Kick."

"Stop right there," smile Rego. "Harry, read it all. I want to hear it all just one more time."

Harry hoped the paper would hold together.

And as he looked at Rego, he could see that Rego was reliving the good old days in Rego's home when the radio told it all.

Harry hoped to sound like Graham MacNamee or Ted Husing just for Rego's sake.

"Rego Kicks Extra Point to Save Game."

"State made two great scoring marches of 71 and 44 yards in a demonstration of brutal offensive power, but it had to depend on Johnny Rego's place-kick conversion to give it a 13 to 12 victory over Western State in a gripping football struggle here Saturday.

"For Western State, finding holes in the State defense, put on one great scoring march of its own, which, with a touchdown pass, matched State touchdowns.

"But the Wildmen couldn't add a point conversion and by that heartbreaking margin joined the list of the nation's defeated elevens.

Leo T. McCall

"As State ground its way along the victory path for its fifth in a row, it set the stage for settling the Big Nine title when it meets the Wolfs Saturday.

"The Wolfs and State alone are undefeated in the Big Nine.

"The State-Wildmen struggle was worthy of the top position it held on the week's schedule. It kept a near capacity throng of almost 50,000 spectators breathless to the finish."

Harry became so wrapped up in the report of this long-forgotten game that he didn't notice Rego starting to struggle for breath.

So he read on:

"There never was one minute of the 60 when the game couldn't have swung either way. State was never out of danger until the Wildmen threw their final pass with less than two minutes to go.

"This was the first time State had won over the Wildmen on their soil since 1927 and, by whatever the margin, avenged the loss to the Wildmen at State last year.

"Battering Bob Szeigle, the State fullback who played another whale of a game, scored both of State's touchdowns, once from the one foot line and once from the two yard line."

Rego seemed to be smiling as Harry continued with a detailed report of the game.

Harry finished reading the two columns, full page report on the game before he noticed that a nurse had pulled a sheet over Rego's head.

TEN

The Funeral and the Will

Harry died peacefully in his sleep. He died on a train that was peacefully winding its way through Glacier National Park—not too many miles from Harry's Lodge on top of the mountains. He was on his way to Seattle to settle problems caused by his manager there. His manager, Harry McGree, had slugged a patron of a bar who made accusations over Hall and Hall's sales policies. The patron of course was a former Hall and Hall salesman—embittered over what had been done to him while with the company.

Harry was out to help McGree get good lawyers. But he never made it.

McGree never needed the lawyers. But Hall and Hall needed Harry, and the ensuing years proved it.

The scramble for power began before they closed the lid on Harry's casket.

While loyal employees passed by giving Mrs. Hall their condolences, Russ Fender captured the Wats line and called every major stockholder in the company.

He solicited their support.

Les James, meanwhile, clung closely to Mrs. Hall. For her had had made all the funeral arrangements, notified all of Harry's relatives, contacted the funeral director, arranged for the flowers, sought out the burial grounds.

"Nellie," he said, "Death is a necessary end, it will come when it will come."

Leo T. McCall

Few knew that Les could quote Shakespeare. Nellie thought Les had made it up.

"Les, you know the right thing to say at the right time. How can I thank you enough?"

"Nellie, you know what I thought of Harry. The least I can do is watch over his family in this, their greatest hour of need," smiled Less in a fatherly fashion.

"It will go on. Momentum will carry it. Harry started an organization no one can catch up to in our field," assured Les.

"But someone has to run it. Someone has got to have the final say in all the decisions. Who? Who?"

"Well, I must admit, Harry prepared no one for his demise. He had looked. God knows he had looked. But, being Harry, he never found or even wanted to find anyone. Isn't this true, Nellie?"

As they stood over the casket, Nellie shed a tear or two, but not more. It even seemed she breathed a sigh of relief.

Les noticed it.

"Was he as hard on you as he was on the men?"

"Les, when Harry said he married his job, he meant it. I was a showcase."

Les smiled gently.

"He dreamed of being a ranch boss. He always slept in the bunk out hear the horses."

"Is this why you objected to his being buried in a cemetery? Why you insisted his plot of ground be near the horse barn?"

"It's the only reason. He'd have it no other way."

Harry had given a lot of money to the "needy" —not the beggar on the street, not the poor in the slums, and not to the friend in need of "just one more drink."

He gave where people would hear about it.

He had made headlines in local newspapers yearly with:

Business Is Baloney

HARRY HALL GIVES $25,000 TO UNITED FUND!

HARRY HALL DONATES $50,000 TO NEIGHBORHOOD PLAYGROUND!

HARRY HALL PLEDGES $35,000 to RED CROSS!

HARRY HALL FOOTS ALL OF BILL FOR CHARITY BALL!

HARRY HALL KICKS OFF NEW HOSPITAL DRIVE WITH $100,000!

HARRY HALL OFFERS 20 ACRES OF PROPERTY FOR COMMUNITY PLAYGROUND!

HARRY HALL BUILDS $250,000 WING FOR THE LITTLE SISTERS OF THE POOR HOME!

Hall and Hall stood behind all of these pledges and promises and made them come true. But *Harry* carried away all the honors and trophies.

So, streaming by the casket, came the Director of the United Fund, Directors of the Neighborhood Playground, Director of the Red Cross, and last but not least, a few nuns who came to offer up Harry's soul to the poor souls in purgatory.

"Your husband was a great man, Mrs. Hall," wept a grateful Poor Sister. She then very gently placed a Rosary made of roses on Harry's dead chest.

"If it were not for Harry Hall, our hospital would never have been possible," firmly stated Mrs. Smith, the head of the hospital drive.

"So goes a great man," Les James commented occasionally and from time to time knelt by the body and wept.

No great actress or no great actor can hope to duplicate the performances given by Harry Hall's friends.

A few came in honest sorrow, actually sorry to see Harry dead. Others came just to make sure Harry was dead.

No one knew if Coach Yeno (an old friend of his Como gang) was sorry or intensely happy to see Harry dead.

"Mrs. Hall, I am deeply sorry to see the end of a great career, the end of all of us of a great humanitarian. No one knew him better than you and I. He lived a full life. He passed away with his boots on. That's the way he wanted it. He died a peaceful death. Let us hope that someday you and I can do the same."

Coach Yeno then puffed his pipe and slipped away into the crowd.

Fender was no different. His words were almost the same. The always smiling Fender now drooped at the corners of his mouth. Furrows dug deep into his forehead.

"Mrs. Hall, you know Harry gave me my start. You know what I thought of him. You know how deeply sorry I am to see him pass into the unknown. And as Harry always said: 'Someday the man upstairs will stop my heart and make me go upstairs and shut the door.' The day ahs come, Mrs. Hall. He sleeps peacefully after a job well done. May the same happen to you and me some day."

Fender kissed her tenderly on the cheek and passed on into the crowd. As he did he hugged all three of Harry's children.

"If you need a father now, you know where I am."

Joe Miller, Harry's chauffeur, handled his part like he was at an Irish wake. At least he was true to form.

"It is a wonderful thing, Mrs. Hall...death. Look at it this way: You're born to live and you're born to die. It's cigars for babies—champagne for the bride and groom (and seeing the rosary of roses on Harry's chest) and roses for the dead."

Eloquently, Miller continued:

"Ashes to ashes and dust to dust. Harry's riding off into the sunset like the Lone Ranger in a cloud of dust."

Mrs. Hall look startled at the thought.

Miller continued:

Business Is Baloney

"I regret that Harry died in his sleep. He would rather have gone down the road fighting Coach Yeno tooth and nail, chastising Fender, wailing away at me—but in his sleep never. I say never!"

The truth Mrs. Hall did not need at this time.

Mrs. Miller could see it and grabbed Miller by the arm and led him firmly away into the crowd.

"I told you you're not at an Irish wake. You can't see that?"

"What are they trying to make of this wake? A funeral? I say it's time for a great celebration!" said Miller.

Miller dragged her husband out of Mrs. Hall's earshot before she could pick up Miller's last remark.

Russ Fender stood back in a corner of the funeral parlor. Ever since he ruined the Barbecue, he had stood in disfavor with Harry. Harry never demoted him.

Miller came just to make sure he was dead. He had already made his plans to leave the company now that Harry died. He knew he couldn't get more pay anywhere else or as much as Harry paid him. So he had stayed as long as he could. Any successor to Harry would find out Fender was carried for many years just because "Harry liked him" —not because of anything he could do. Harry knew it. Only the favors Fender did and the applause he gave Harry on numerous occasions, induced Harry to keep him on the payroll.

Nothing too eventful happened during the burial.

The pallbearers were the six whom Harry had strung along for so many years.

At the ranch they took Harry's body from the hearse.

Russ Fender and Joe Miller were in the two lead positions on the casket. In the middle came Coach Yeno and Les James. Bringing up the rear, puffing heavily and straining to hold the casket up, stumbled Tommy Ribbon and Harry's lawyer, Leo Openhaus. Mrs. Hall, in a black dress, black shoes, black stockings and a black veil, followed the casket to a plot by the horse barn. A few horses stood around during the burial ceremony.

Leo Openhaus, the only highly educated man in the organization, had been chosen by Harry many years before Harry's death to give the eulogy, should be, Harry, die before him.

So there, beside the ranch house, in the quiet of the evening, in the presence of a handful of people, the remains of Harry Hall were gently lowered to his ranch yard grave. Openhaus gave the eulogy which turned out to be Harry's will. He read:

> "Under the wide and starry sky
> Dig the grave and let me lie.
> Glad did I live and gladly die,
> And I laid me down with a will."

"Ladies and Gentlemen," continued Openhaus. "You will note the little requiem and eulogy I have just read is by the learned and renowned poet Robert Louis Stevenson. Let me read the last sentence again. And I laid me down with a *will*."

"Yes—and I laid me down with a *will*."

"I see no need to call this gathering together again. Harry laid himself down with a will which I will read now. I see no need to call this gathering together again. Everyone involved in the will is here." Openhaus cleared his throat.

"It hardly seemed like the appropriate time. But Harry in life never put off any decisions and in death he wouldn't want us to do the same."

Leo Openhaus dug into his brief case. There in the dusk of the evening, he turned the will to catch the last rays of the sun and read it.

Business Is Baloney

"I, Harry Hall, being of sound body and mind do hereby bequest all my money, estate, stocks and bonds and other valuable goods to the following:

1. Coach Yeno...my Sterling Silver Saddle.
2. To Tommy Ribbon...my buckskin and high heel boots.
3. To Les James...my pearl-handled revolvers.
4. To Russ Fender...my diamond-studded lighter.
5. To Joe Miller...my Cadillac.

Openhaus read on and on as Harry bequeathed various personal goods to loyal employees that had served faithfully and well. Money he did not give away.

As the will was read, Miller, Harrigan and Fender wept openly. James comforted Mrs. Hall.

Openhaus read on:

"To the City College I bequeath a trust fund of ten million dollars. Any and all funds shall be used only in the erection of new buildings. Such buildings when erected shall have carved in stone over the main entrance—made to last as long as the building itself—the name...Harry Hall. For example: If it is to be a Liberal Arts building it shall read: THE HARRY HALL LIBERAL ARTS BUILDING. If it to be an athletic field it shall read: THE HARRY HALL STADIUM. If it should be a Science building it shall read: THE HARRY HALL HALL OF SCIENCE. If it should be a school of law it shall read: THE HARRY HALL SCHOOL OF LAW. If it should be a school of medicine it shall read: HARRY HALL SCHOOL OF MEDICINE."

Leo T. McCall

On and on, Openhaus read every possible building that could be erected at City College in the foreseeable future with Harry's name to be carved on it. The will covered every possible building, A to Z, from the School of Agriculture to the Department of Zoology.

"All the rest of my possessions, my stock in Hall and Hall included, are bequeathed to my wife."

"And that, gentlemen, is Harry Hall's will. For obvious reasons I have not read the sums of how much money Harry has in banks, how much stock h e controls in other companies, the worth of his estate, etc. etc. etc. I believe these personal to Mrs. Hall alone, and that Harry wouldn't want me to divulge them for public perusal."

Les James helped Mrs. Hall back into her car and then drove her back to the main house. Fender, Coach Yeno, Henders, Ribbon and Openhaus departed in their own cars.

The sun dropped behind the hills. Darkness began to settle over the ranch.

And day was done.

About the Author

Leo T. McCall graduated from the University of St. Thomas in St. Paul, MN. Currently he is employed as an advertising salesman for the Perlich Co. in St. Paul and District Manager of the Universal Photonics Company out of Hicksville, New York.

With a B.A. in English he started his career as an English teacher in a local St. Paul High School. Most of his career has been spent in business as a credit manager, sales manager, and advertising specialist. His career is as varied as the speech he gave while acting Jacques in "As You Like It" by Shakespeare, to whit "All the world is a stage…each man plays many parts." His career can be summed up from a copy of what his grandson said about him:

My grandpa, Leo "the lion" McCall, has had many occupations, interests, and hobbies in his lifetime. When my grandpa was six years old, he got up at five o'clock in the morning to deliver papers. Rain or shine, freezing or hot, he would deliver. He did this until he was twelve, and he still takes great pride in it. He also says that he had to throw coal in the furnace when he woke up, and he had to feed the dog before he left. Later, in the nineteen forties, he taught English at Cretin High School. My grandfather loved English, especially Shakespeare. He only taught there for a year, and then went on to work for the F.B.I. He was too good of a field agent, so they moved him to the fingerprint department, and that is all the information I am allowed to release. From the F.B.I he moved on to work for Brown and Bigelow, and he was a very good salesman. He still is a salesman, but now he works for Michael Sales Company. My grandpa loves to write. He writes poems, plays, books, and almost everything! He is now currently writing a book about his life. He has been working on it for about two years. Since my grandmother died two years ago, he has picked up some new interests, one of which is cooking. He loves to bake pies. He makes one or two a week, and passes them out to clients, family, and friends. His pies are better than Bakers Square, and so he always has a waiting list for recipients. My grandfather loves to golf. He passed his golf knowledge and talent on to my dad, and then my dad passed it on to me. Another interest of his is crossword puzzles. He works on one puzzle every day and he can usually finish every one. This has been my paragraph about my grandpa who is very special to me and is a very interesting person.

Brian McCall

Brian McCall

8040

Printed in the United States
881200001B

NORMANDALE COMMUNITY COLLEGE
LIBRARY
9700 FRANCE AVENUE SOUTH
BLOOMINGTON, MN 55431-4399